D0457112

THREE CROSS

Shawn Starbuck had covered thousands of rugged miles through the wild Southwest, in search of his lost brother Ben. Now at last, he had a real clue. The end seemed almost in sight . . .

Then Starbuck met up with Jim Kelso, a man who desperately needed his help. Kelso's ranch, Three Cross, was besieged by ruthless marauders who would stop at nothing until the ranch was theirs. What were they after? What was the priceless secret of Three Cross? Starbuck swore to find out, though it might mean losing the trail to Ben—and his own neck—in a blood-drenched battle for land and gold.

Ray Hogan is an author who has inspired a loyal following over the years since he published his first Western novel *Ex-marshal* in 1956. Hogan was born in Willow Springs, Missouri, where his father was town marshal. At five the Hogan family moved to Albuquerque where Ray Hogan still lives in the foothills of the Sandia and Manzano mountains. His father was on the Albuquerque police force and, in later years, owned the Overland Hotel. It was while listening to his father and other old-timers tell tales from the past that Ray was inspired to recast these tales in fiction. From the beginning he did exhaustive research into the history and the people of the Old West and the walls of his study are lined with various firearms, spurs, pictures, books, and memorabilia, about all of which he can talk in dramatic detail. Among his most popular works are the series of books about Shawn Starbuck, a searcher in a quest for a lost brother, who has a clear sense of right and wrong and who is willing to stand up and be counted when it is a question of fairness or justice. His other major series is about lawman John Rye whose reputation has earned him the sobriquet The Doomsday Marshal. 'I've attempted to capture the courage and bravery of those men and women that lived out West and the dangers and problems they had to overcome,' Hogan once remarked. If his lawmen protagonists seem sometimes larger than life, it is because they are men of integrity, heroes who through grit of character and common sense are able to overcome the obstacles they encounter despite often overwhelming odds. This same grit of character can also be found in Hogan's heroines and, in *The Vengeance of Fortuna West*, Hogan wrote a gripping and totally believable account of a woman who takes up the badge and tracks the men who killed her lawman husband by ambush. No less intriguing in her way is Nellie Dupray, convicted of rustling in *The Glory Trail*. Above all, what is most impressive about Hogan's Western novels is the consistent quality with which each is crafted, the compelling depth of his characters, and his ability to juxtapose the complexities of human conflict into narratives always as intensely interesting as they are emotionally involving. His latest novel is *Soldier in Buckskin*.

THREE CROSS

Ray Hogan

GUNSMOKE

This hardback edition 2006
by BBC Audiobooks Ltd
by arrangement with
Golden West Literary Agency

ISBN 10: 1 4056 8099 7
ISBN 13: 978 1 405 68099 8

British Library Cataloguing in Publication Data available.

Printed and bound in Great Britain by
Antony Rowe Ltd., Chippenham, Wiltshire

═ 1 ═

Near the crest of the butte, Starbuck pulled his horse to a halt, eying a sleek, golden eagle, which sprang gracefully into the shimmering layers of heat hovering over the flat below, and on powerful wings began to climb into the sky.

He continued to watch as the great, russet-colored bird leveled off, slipped into a long glide toward the pinnacled Organ Mountains, rising in somber grandeur on the yonder side of Las Cruces, yet a half day's ride in the distance. Then, lowering his gaze in deference to the glare, he shifted wearily on the saddle, brushed at the sweat accumulated on his face. A few moments later, as if suddenly deciding to indulge himself, he swung down, sighing gratefully as his heels hit the solid assurance of the ground. Leaving the chestnut gelding to tear at the scattered tufts of browned grass, he crossed slowly to a nearby turret of wind-scourged granite and leaned his lank shape against its shaded side.

Again he grunted softly, contentedly. It had been a long ride—ten straight days—since he'd mounted the gelding at Lynchburg where he had gone on what had developed into just another fruitless errand in his search for his brother, Ben. Now, following out still another tip, he was heading for the old settlement of The Crosses in the lower end of New Mexico Territory.

He was acting on strange and somewhat disturbing information. A man, skilled in boxing, was wanted for murder by the sheriff of that town. Their father, Hiram, an expert in the art who could have become a professional champion had he loved the land less and fame more, had tutored his two sons to a level of near perfection. . . . Thus the man sought could be Ben since masters of the science were few along the frontier.

But Ben a murderer—a killer?

Shawn found that part difficult to accept—not that Ben wasn't capable of violent anger; his fiery temper had been one of the principal factors in the break between him and old Hiram that led to his leaving home ten long years ago. It contributed also to the reason why Shawn, now seeking his brother in order to settle the Starbuck estate, was having so hard a time tracking him down; not only was he searching for a man he'd not seen in a decade but also one who undoubtedly lived under an assumed name.

But the need to find Ben was absolute, and while the trails that carried Shawn back and forth across the western frontier seemed to have no ending, merely brief pauses during which frustration and disappointment were his only rewards, he knew he could never stop the quest until he found Ben or knew positively that he was dead. Such was his destiny; he had long since come to recognize that fact.

Las Cruces, however, must necessarily be home for a while. He didn't expect to find Ben there, only hoped to get himself a job, rebuild his depleted cash, and he would garner all information possible from the lawman—a good description perhaps and, hopefully, the name Ben was now living under, if indeed the person in question was his brother.

Pausing to work periodically was no new experience to Shawn Starbuck. Hiram, in setting forth in his will that his younger son must first find and return to the fold the offended Ben, had overlooked the fact that money would be needed to carry on the search; or perhaps the elder Starbuck had figured Ben would be somewhere close-by and easily located, and therefore made no provision for expense. The lawyer in charge of the estate had remedied the situation somewhat by granting Shawn enough cash to get started, but it had only lasted for a few months.

After that it became a matter, a system actually, of alternately searching and working and then searching again until the money he had saved ran out and once more it became necessary to find a job for a time. Shawn had acquired a wealth of experience, both good and bad, pursuing such a program. It had converted him from an affable, somewhat unripe, gray-eyed farm boy a few months past eighteen years of age in the beginning, to a lean, trail-hardened man most thought twice about before challenging. It showed in his overall appearance—one that belied the disarming boyish way he had of smiling when pleased; it showed in the slant of the smooth-handled pistol worn on his left side, the easy, yet coiled slouch to his carriage—in the utterly direct and uncompromising manner he had of looking at a man from below a shelf of dark, full brows.

No less characteristic were the creases in his element-ravaged face—the hard, strong lines cut there by the sun, the sweeping winds, the cold rains—all bespeaking the patience of the man and his unwillingness to admit defeat that, many times when his mood was black, presented itself. . . . He'd never find his brother, a sly voice told him at such moments; Ben could be dead, buried under a false name—and even if alive the land was too vast, too remote for him to find traces of one solitary individual.

He could waste a lifetime—a lifetime during which he might have settled down, built for himself a world of his own, found peace and contentment. "Hunting Ben," someone encountered along the road somewhere, sometime, had said to him, "was like trying to rope a cloud, saddle a moonbeam; it was a hopeless task."

And there were those dreary moments in which Shawn was close to agreement, but there was inside him a quality inherited from Clare, his schoolteacher mother, or perhaps passed on to him by iron-jawed, hard-fisted old Hiram—a stubbornness that would not let him give up, admit failure. He would find Ben, clear up the estate, and claim his rightful share—thirty thousand dollars—and then seek the life he knew awaited him. It might take—

The sound of horses moving along the base of the butte caught his attention. The muted voices of men came to him then, and pulling away from the rock upthrust he made his way toward the lip of the formation and the lightning-struck charred cedar upon which the eagle had been perched when frightened by the approach of the gelding. He moved quietly, carefully. He had successfully avoided parties of renegade Apaches all the way from Lynchburg, and he'd like the record to remain unsullied.

Peering over the rim he saw they were not Apaches; four riders dressed in ordinary range clothing, with the exception that each wore a large, triangularly folded scarf around his neck in addition to the customary bandana cowhands used as protection against dust and the sun.

Shawn watched them pass in single file, cut down into a sandy, brush-lined arroyo, and angle toward the south. Mexico lay in that direction—a long forty miles distant. He frowned, considering that. Riders heading for the border would more than likely stick to the shaded path of the Rio Grande where traveling would be more pleasant, rather than buck the endless, dry flats where the heat was known to go well above a hundred degrees.

Casting his glance ahead of the riders, now moving steadily away, Starbuck's eyes picked up the tan ribbon of highway lying a mile or so farther on. This would be the main road from Las Cruces, Mesilla, and points east, and which led on to Lordsburg, Tucson, and finally to San

7

Francisco; and incidentally, the route of the Butterfield stagecoaches, he realized.

Turned thoughtful by that, he scanned the upper and lower stretches of the curving, undulating strip through eyes narrowed to cut down the glare. It could be a holdup in the making.

That assumption abruptly crystallized into conviction. Off to his left a yellow cloud began to boil up, take shape. It was the stage—a few hours out of Las Cruces on its westward journey. Starbuck cut his gaze back to the four riders. They were keeping to the arroyo, moving on a direct line of interception.

Shawn murmured an oath. He'd hoped to reach the settlement well before dark, but here was interruption, something luck seemed to enjoy plaguing him with during his search for Ben. It shouldn't be necessary for him to step in, help prevent the crime; the government had troops garrisoned at nearby Fort Cummings for just this purpose —protecting travelers from road-agents and Apaches. . . . Where the hell were they, anyway? Probably doing close-order drill on the parade ground at the whim of some shavetail weighted down by the shiny new bars on his shoulders. No matter, they army wasn't around and that left it squarely up to him.

Turning, he moved back for the gelding. It wasn't that he disliked helping others; actually, he'd more or less grown accustomed to the frequent impromptu demands of the beleagured that he encounered since the search for Ben had begun; but it seemed such occasions always presented themselves at the most inopportune times.

Jaw taut, he reached the chestnut and swung to the saddle. Slicing off the upper end of the formation, and keeping the rocks between the four riders and himself, he rode down into the arroyo. There, ignoring the deeply imprinted tracks left by the outlaws' horses in the loose sand, he set out to follow.

In a short time he caught sight of them. They were now riding abreast and moving more slowly, evidently pointing for another series of buttes just ahead. He could not see the road from where he was but guessed it proably ran along the back side of the squat, brushy formations.

Maintaining a safe distance, Starbuck watched the men veer to the right, dip into a narrow ravine, and disappear. At once he spurred the chestnut, curving to his left in order to keep from being seen. At the lip of the wash he drew up, slipped quietly to the ground, and edged forward to where he could look into the ravine.

The riders were just below. They were sitting their mounts, making ready for the holdup. One, a large man with a sweat-stained black hat, was examining his pistol, twirling the cylinder, slipping the hammer, assuring himself the weapon was loaded and in working order. He paused, glanced sideways to one of companions.

"You got it straight, Kid—he's on this stage for certain."

It was a statement more than a question. The Kid, much younger than the others, had blond, stringy hair that bushed down over his collar. There was a nervousness to him as if he were new to the calling.

"I'm sure, Dallman, I'm sure," he answered in an offended tone. "He's heading for Tucson. Carrying the money with him—five thousand gold."

"You all'd best keep your eyes peeled for that there guard," the rider on a dapple-gray said, fitting his black scarf across the lower half of his face. "Prob'ly be old George Eberhardt—and he's a real stem-winding sonofabitch with that there scatter-gun of his."

"Not if he collects hisself a bullet right between the eyes before he gets the chance," Dallman said drily, and glanced over his shoulder to the fourth outlaw. "Ain't that a fact, Charlie?"

Charlie, a narrow-shouldered man with a rifle cradled in his arms, bobbed, spat a stream of brown juice at a nearby rock.

"Just you leave him to me. . . . Got myself a little score I'm aiming to mark off. He winged me once with that goddammed scatter-gun. Still got sore spots on my ass when I set a saddle. . . . Going to pick him off that seat like he was a crow a setting on a rail fence."

"Well," Dallman said, sliding his pistol back into its leather, "don't get yourself so fired up remembering, that you miss. I ain't honing to get my head blowed off by no half a bucket of buckshot."

"Me—I don't never miss—"

"She's about here," the Kid announced, standing up in his stirrups and looking toward the advancing roll of dust. "Where you wanting me to hide?"

Dallman surveyed the shallow cove before him. "Charlie, you get yourself over there next them rocks at the corner of the bluff, like you figured . . . Kid, expect you'd best keep this side of him. Waldo—you find yourself a place on the right. Means I'll be in the middle so's I can work both sides. Savvy?"

"Si senor," the one called Waldo said in exaggerated Spanish and swung away from the others.

Starbuck turned quickly, retraced his steps to the chestnut. He'd delayed too long to throw down on the quartet while they were together in a group; likely it wouldn't have been smart. Men such as Dallman and his kind ordinarily felt they were living on borrowed time anyway, and took any and all chances to prolong their fragile tenure on life.

Going to the saddle, he cut left and gained a small rise. From there he could see the coach drawing nearer on the road, swaying and rocking on its thorough braces as the six-horse hitch thundered up the slight grade. There were the usual two men on the seat—the driver and a guard, both grizzled oldsters who'd likely made the run many times, knew every bend and turn, and had learned long ago to be ready for anything.

The roll curtains had been lowered in the coach to cut out the sun and discourage the dust that swirled up from the spinning wheels, thus Shawn was unable to see how many passengers were aboard. . . . One at least—the man traveling to Tucson with five thousand dollars in gold.

Spurring the chestnut off the knoll and down the slope, Starbuck cut a straight line for the oncoming vehicle, rapidly drawing in range of the outlaws' ambush.

= 2 =

He saw reaction to his appearance immediately. The driver yelled something at the guard—George Eberhardt the outlaws had called him—who laid aside his shotgun and reached down for a rifle lying at his feet.

Shawn, both hands above his head, palms flat and forward, motioned for the driver to pull up. The reply to his request was quick. George opened up with the rifle, and the driver, leaning forward, began to ply the whip to his team. Bullets dug into the sand around the gelding's hooves or droned angrily by. Starbuck swore, began to slow. Evidently this particular stretch of road had witnessed more than its share of holdups and George and the driver were taking no chances.

But they were heading into sure and certain trouble, an encounter that was designed to be fatal for Eberhardt, and would likely prove to be so for the driver and his passenger as well. . . . But somehow the holdup must be prevented, Shawn realized, ignoring the impulse to forget the whole damned affair and let George and his hasty trigger finger cope with the problem.

Again roweling the chestnut, he sent the big horse toward the coach, this time removing his hat and waving it frantically back and forth with one hand while pointing at the buttes with the other. The old guard stubbornly continued to lever his rifle, and as the distance between them narrowed, the slugs began to strike closer.

Disgusted, Starbuck pulled off into a side gully. It was sheer suicide to try and stop the coach. He'd have to accept the alternative—that of riding on ahead and springing the outlaws' trap before the stage could reach that point.

Pivoting the foam-flecked gelding, he used spurs once more, lined out down the draw for the row of squat bluffs. It would have been so much simpler, and evidently far safer, to have moved in on the outlaws from above when he had looked down upon them and heard them make their plans. The four of them could not have posed any greater threat than did old George Eberhardt and the rifle he made such persistent use of. . . . But it was too late to think of that now; the coach was near and there was but one thing left for him to do—ride in ahead of it, hope to catch Dallman and the others by surprise.

He did have one advantage denied the coach and anyone else keeping to the road; he could hug the base of the buttes, taking protection from the rocks and the bulging shoulders of red earth. Such would permit him to work in close to the outlaws before being spotted. Undoubtedly they were now wondering just what all the shooting was about.

Eberhardt had ceased his use of the rifle and that was a relief. Either the guard was assuming he had turned back a would-be road agent, or doubt had seeped into his mind as to the actual intent of the rider who had sought to flag down the stage. In either event he was now simply watching and waiting.

Shawn looked beyond the chestnut's cocked ears. Charlie would be posted at an outermost wedge of rocks jutting from the front of the first butte. The others would be strung out in a more or less curved line across the cove. Dallman and the two with him would simply hold back until Charlie got in his promised deadly shot, and then all would converge on the coach as the driver, no longer with protection, would be forced to brake his horses to a stop.

Charlie, therefore, was the key to the situation; he must be downed before he could use his weapon. Shawn probed the rocky outcropping with squinted eyes. The outlaw should be at the forward edge where he would have an unobstructed view of the stagecoach's approach. . . . His nerves tightened. He must get to that point as quickly as possible; he would be running a long chance—that of unexpectedly coming face to face with the outlaw and braving a split-second shoot out with him. If he were lucky he'd get off the first bullet; if not—well, he'd played the cards he'd been dealt.

Drawing his pistol he thumbed back the hammer, pulled the chestnut down to a fast walk. There was no sign yet of Charlie, nor of the other outlaws, but they could not be far off; the hollowed out area in the bluffs was just ahead.

He glanced to the road. The coach was dipping into a swale, the plunging horses running at top speed, manes flying, mouths gaped to the sawing of the bits. Eberhardt was hunched forward, rifle or shotgun, whichever, across his bony knees. The driver, whip curling out over the backs of his team, was a ramrod-straight figure beside him.

Charlie. . . .

12

The outlaw was before Starbuck abruptly. It was as if he'd turned the corner of a building and walked directly into the man. Shawn saw the startled look on the man's bearded face, saw the blur and glint as he pivoted to use the rifle held in his hands. Instinctively he threw his weight to the right side of the saddle and triggered his pistol. The explosions of the two weapons came together as an identical blast.

Starbuck felt the bullet whip at the slack in his sleeve, heard it slam against the rocks now behind him and scream eerily off into space. Charlie, on his feet and twisting slowly, was frowning darkly. He stared at Shawn for a long moment and then took a faltering step backwards. An instant later he was gone, dropping from sight as he went over the ledge on which he had crouched, down into the gully below.

Starbuck wheeled. Already the remaining outlaws, recovered from their surprise, were sweeping toward him from the depths of the cove. Guns began to hammer. Bullets thudded into the rocks beyond him, spurting sand over the chestnut's hooves. He cut sharp again. A rider loomed up immediately to his right, coming in from the ravine into which Charlie had fallen. Shawn snapped a shot at the man, missed, pressed off a second. The outlaw—Waldo, Starbuck recognized him in that next fleeting instant—buckled forward as his horse slowed, and then fell from his saddle.

Eberhardt opened up from his position on the road, the heavier crack of the rifle distinct above the sharp, quick reports of pistols. Shawn again changed course, realizing the two remaining outlaws, Dallman and the Kid, were somewhere on the far side of the cove—that the stagecoach guard apparently had them pinned down.

He spurred the gelding, broke into the open, praying that Eberhardt would not mistake him for one of the outlaws and start pumping lead in his direction. Strangely, at that precise instant, all shooting ceased. From the tail of his eye he saw the coach slowing to a halt, and then far to his right he caught a glimpse of Dallman and the blond Kid, topping out a ridge as they raced off to safety.

Sighing, Starbuck mopped at the sweat covering his face. It had worked out better than he'd had reason to hope. Pulling the chestnut about, he walked the gelding through the drifting dust and smoke toward the vehicle, now at a stand-still in the road. The driver, a wiry, elderly man with a bristly moustache and leather gauntlets that reached almost to his elbows, greeted him with a smile.

13

"Sure obliged to you, mister! Appears we was running smack dab into a ambush!"

Shawn nodded, again brushing at the moisture clouding his eyes. He glanced at Eberhardt. "Tried to warn you but your guard—"

Instantly George Eberhardt was on his feet. "Now, how in blazes was I supposed to know what you was up to?" he demanded testily. Like the driver he was lean, sharp-faced, and well up in years; unlike his partner, there was an irritability to him, an impatient sort of petulance. "You figure me for a mind reader?"

Starbuck shrugged indifferently. "Doubt if any road-agent would be fool enough to ride straight into you the way I was doing."

"Just what I told him, dammit!" the driver said vehemently. "But ain't nobody never told George Eberhardt nothing—no, sir! Never!"

"My job is to keep this here coach from getting held up," the guard countered. "I ain't about to take no chances when I ain't sure of nothing."

"Maybe, but a man ought to use some horse sense—"

Shawn smiled, wondering if the two oldsters fiddled away the miles between stage stops with continuous bickering. He shifted his attention to the coach. The curtains had been rolled up. The door opened and a well-dressed man stepped out. Starbuck could see two other figures inside but they made no move to dismount. Women, he thought. . . . The passenger came toward him.

"Name's Winston. Regardless of what the guard and driver have to say, I'm obliged to you," he said in a deep toned voice. "A holdup would have been a disastrous experience for me."

From the man's appearance and manner of speaking, he was an easterner; going to California to invest, build himself a fortune, Shawn guessed. He'd heard things were really booming up San Francisco way.

"Expect it would," he said. "Next time you plan to carry a lot of gold with you, best you take pains to keep it quiet.

Winston frowned, glanced to the driver, to the guard, and then came back to Starbuck. "I—I don't understand how—"

"One word's all it takes. Somebody overhears it, adds up a couple of things—and you've got a holdup waiting down the road."

"Must have been it—that saloon last night. Town where

14

we stayed—Mesilla. Just happened to mention where I was going—plans I had—"

"That was it," Starbuck said, and rode in closer to the coach. Looking up at the two men on the seat, he jerked a thumb in the direction of the dead outlaws. "Can't leave them there for the buzzards. Mind helping me boost them onto their horses so's I—"

"Got a better idea," the driver broke in. "Boot's empty, or nigh onto it. We'll load them aboard, haul them to the next way station. Can bury them there. . . . Might save you a passel of trouble."

"Suits me fine," Starbuck said, happy to be relieved of taking the bodies to Las Cruces and making the necessary explanations to the sheriff. Occasionally, in such instances, complications arose that caused a man, doing only what he considered his public duty, considerable grief. "Might as well tie on their horses, too."

"Why not?" the old driver said, gathering up the lines and kicking off his brake. "Something a stage line can always use is horses," he added as he cut the coach about and headed it toward the cove.

Pulling up halfway between the two outlaws, he again locked the wheels, and then climbed down. Starbuck, ground reining the chestnut, moved toward the ravine where Charlie lay. The older man followed, paused suddenly, and flung a speculative look at Eberhardt.

"You hamstrung, or something? We can use a mite of help."

George wagged his head. "I ain't stirring off this here vehicle. I'm not forgetting two of them owlhoots got plumb away."

The driver shrugged. "Ain't likely they'll come back—not with two of their partners dead. But suit yourself," he said and hurried to overtake Shawn.

Together they loaded the bodies into the baggage compartment in the rear of the coach, and then, catching up the loose horses, tied them to the axle.

Dusting himself off with his hat, the driver nodding to Starbuck said, "Again sure want to thank you, friend. Was a good turn you done us. Old George there thanks you too, only it just ain't his way to be beholden."

Shawn smiled and extended his hand. "Lucky I came along at the right time."

"For us it sure was, maybe not for them two in the back. They had us cold, then you showed up. . . . Where you heading—say, reckon I forgot my manners in all this here hullabaloo. I'm Henry Mason."

15

"Starbuck—Shawn Starbuck. I'm riding to Las Cruces. Got to find myself a job."

Mason pursed his lips, clucked softly. "I ain't in 'Cruces much so I don't know whether jobs around there are scarce or not. Most places, seems they are. . . . Wish't I could steer you on to something, but, like I said—"

"Looking for my brother, too. Name's Ben, but it's likely he's not going by that." Shawn had made it a hard and fast rule to always ask, make inquiry. There was always a slim chance—the hope—

He was aware of Mason's curious expression. "Then how can you find—"

"Think he might look something like me. Maybe a bit shorter and heavier. Got reason to think he was around this neck of the woods a year or so ago—in Las Cruces, probably. Could have put on a boxing exhibition. Maybe you'll remember him from that."

"That what you are—one of them boxer fellows?" Mason asked, leathery features lighting with interest as he pointed to the engraved silver belt buckle that Shawn was wearing, with the superimposed ivory figure of a trained fighter centered on it.

"My pa taught us both. The buckle was his. Friends gave it to him. You remember seeing a man in town that put on a boxing show who might've looked a little like me?"

Mason's shoulders stirred. "Sure don't, but like I said, I ain't in 'Cruces much. Sometimes I ain't around for a week or more. Could've happened and me being away, I wouldn't knowed a thing about it. . . . When you get there, look up Abel Morrison. He's the sheriff. He'll recollect."

Shawn nodded, turned to the chestnut. Morrison might remember—and only too well. It appeared, however, that the lawman was going to be his best bet. Swinging to the saddle, he raised his hand in salute to Eberhardt, to Winston, peering out of the coach window, to Henry Mason, climbing back onto his seat and taking up the leathers.

"Luck—" he called.

"Same to you," the driver shouted back, and sent his team lunging against their harness with a sharp command.

Eberhardt twisted about, lifting his gloved hand almost reluctantly. "Sure was a nice fellow," he admitted. "Seems I've seen him before, somewheres."

"More'n just nice!" Mason snorted. "Know what he told me? That there road-agent that was holed up at the point was laying for you special. Said he had a score to settle.

16

Something about you filling his backside with buckshot once."

George scrubbed at his ear. "Done that to plenty of yahoos in my time of being a shotgun rider. Never got no look at him. We get to the station, I'll have me a gander."

"And about him looking familiar—he's here hunting his brother—name of Ben Starbuck."

Eberhardt continued to claw at his ear while he repeated the name slowly. Finally he shook his head. "Nope, don't ring no bells. What was this boy called?"

"Shawn—Shawn Starbuck."

"Well, I ever see him again I'll ask him about this brother of his'n—and where maybe I could've seen him."

"Might've done that back there, polite like, and sort of paid back the favor he done us," Mason snapped.

"Just didn't have no chance—"

"Sure you did! Them outlaws wasn't about to come back—and you know it!"

"Don't know nothing of the kind! They could've just been holding off, waiting to catch us not looking. . . . I got to think of things like that—my job."

"Could've watched from the ground—"

"Not good's I could've from up here—"

Mason, with the coach back on the road, his team running smoothly, settled himself on the seat and glanced sideways at the guard.

"Oh, the hell with you," he said affectionately. "Got any more of that chawin' handy?"

3

It was past mid afternoon, with the sun burning in hot for September, when Shawn rode into Las Cruces. Something like a year had elapsed since he was in the settlement clustered along the east bank of the river—the Rio Grande—and he saw little change. But recalling that he had paused there only briefly as he made his way northward from Laredo where he had hoped to find Ben, he reckoned he was not in a position to judge well.

Now, as he halted in the shade of a giant cottonwood at the edge of town, he wondered if this visit would prove any more productive than the first—or all the other places he had journeyed to. He had so little to go on; no name, only a vague idea of personal appearance, and one distinguishing mark—a small scar above the left eye that was all but invisible except at close range.

No one, it seemed, ever took note of the defacement, and likely such was to be expected. Ben had acquired it when they were small boys playing on the rocks their father had dragged in from a field he was clearing. In the years that followed, the mark became covered over by Ben's dark brow, and a man needed to make close examination if he was to find it. Several times Shawn had followed out what appeared to be certain and definite leads based on a scar, only to find when he looked upon the mark that he had failed again. . . . But someday, somewhere, it would end differently.

Wiping sweat from his face and neck, he touched the chestnut lightly with the rowels and moved on down the street, idly glancing at the names of the business houses as he passed. It was habit with him, a subconscious hope, perhaps, that one day he would see somewhere on a window or printed across a signboard, BEN STARBUCK, and the name of his trade or calling.

It was a foolish dream, and he was aware of it. It would never be that easy, for when Ben had left home that day when Hiram Starbuck had thrashed him unmercifully for his failure to perform a given chore, the boy had declared he was through, not only with the parent but with the family name as well. Thus Shawn knew he'd

18

never see a sign or window so lettered. Ben was the stubborn kind and he'd stick to his vow. . . . Still, there was always the chance, the hope. . . .

Amberson's Gun & Saddle Shop . . . Dr. Edwin Christie, Hours at All Times . . . Hunick's General Store . . . Rodriguez Feed & Seed Co. . . . The Golden Horseshoe Saloon, Gambling-Dancing, Gents Welcome . . . Segura's Restaurant . . . The Border City Bank . . . The Amador Hotel— Stable In Rear . . .

That was the only name to awaken memory in Shawn Starbuck's mind. Likely the other merchants had been there too, when he rode through before, but he had taken no notice. He'd spent the night in the Amador—a hostelry erected by a red-headed, blue-eyed Spaniard who gave the place his name, and then, as if reposing small faith in the profit possibilities of an inn, had continued his regular vocation as a freighter, hauling merchandise in and out of Mexico.

It had been a comfortable place to stay the night— cool, friendly, and to young Shawn, just well embarked on the quest for his brother, a welcome relief from the clap-trap hostelries that he'd had occasion to tarry in.

Now, as he swung into the yard at the rear of the building and dismounted, he sighed in anticipation at the prospects of being off the trail, of a good bed, fine meals in a restaurant, and a bit of relaxation in the Spanish Dagger, the saloon which adjoined.

Pulling his rifle from its boot and taking his saddlebags, Starbuck turned the gelding over to the young Mexican who trotted forward from the stable to meet him.

"Take good care of him, *amigo*," he said, fishing into his pocket for a coin. "Tell the hostler I want him rubbed down, grained, and watered slow. Understand?"

The boy nodded, seized the chestnut's reins, and with a shy smile, hurried off toward the adobe brick barn.

Moving on into the Amador's shadowy lobby, Shawn halted at the desk. The clerk, barely noticing his arrival, pushed a pencil and register at him. He wrote *Shawn Starbuck, Lynchburg, Arizona,* in a firm, legible hand, thanks to the schooling his mother had insisted on his getting, and rested himself against the counter.

The clerk handed him a key to which was attached a wooden tag bearing a neatly carved eight, and glanced at the registration. "How long'll you be staying?"

Shawn was looking into the Spanish Dagger, separated from the hotel by a wall in which an arched doorway had

19

been cut for mutual convenience. . . . A beer would taste good, he decided.

"Hard to say," he murmured.

The clerk crossed his arms and settled back patiently. A man in the far corner of the lobby turned the pages of the newspaper he was reading, the sheets making a noisy crackling as he folded them.

"I mean, it depends on how soon I can find myself a job," Starbuck continued, facing the man behind the desk. He wasn't sure if it was the same clerk who had been there before or not. He didn't think so. He had a good memory for such things.

"Know of some rancher around here needing a hand?"

A pained expression crossed the features of the clerk. *Another saddle-bum passing through;* the thought was written in his eyes.

"Nope, sure don't," he replied. "Like to say, it's customary to pay in advance for the room."

None of it was lost on Shawn. Temper lifted slightly within him. "The hell it is," he snapped. "Wasn't when I stopped here before—doubt if it's been changed."

Tossing his saddlebags into a nearby chair and standing his rifle behind it, Starbuck broke the stiffness of his manner with a smile. "I ever take the notion to beat you out of something it'll be for more than a night's lodging."

Turning lazily, he passed through the archway into the darker area of the saloon and crossed to the bar gleaming softly under the lamps. Three or four men were at the tables, and a tall, well-built individual with intense eyes and the rigid carriage of the military was talking to the bartender.

As Starbuck halted, the aproned man said: "Just a minute, Mr. Gentry—got myself a customer," and moved along the back-bar to where he confronted Shawn, question in his manner.

"Make it beer," Shawn said, and laid a coin on the polished surface before him.

The bartender nodded genially, filled the order quickly from the keg partially hidden under the counter.

"You need a refill, sing out," he said and picking up the money, turned away.

Starbuck lifted the mug, had a swallow of the yeasty liquid. It was far from cold but it was refreshing and it relieved the dust-dry coating that lined his throat. He sighed, took a second swing at the glass. . . . Those past ten days or so during which he'd crossed a big chunk of Arizona and a fair sized piece of New Mexico had seemed

20

more lengthy than usual. He supposed it was because he'd had to use such caution in skirting the Antelope Hills and the Cerro Magdalena. Apaches had been reported active in both areas.

"You seen anything of Vern?"

Idly listening, Shawn heard the man called Gentry ask the question of the bartender. . . . One of the men at the table swore loudly, slammed his cards down. The others laughed.

"Sure ain't—leastwise, I've not seen Mr. Ruch since this morning."

Everybody was *mister* to the bartender, it appeared. Shawn guessed for a man in business it was probably a good idea. He helped himself to more beer, considered whether to first pay a call on the sheriff, make inquiries as to work in the valley—and maybe get the conversation swung around to the boxer who was being sought as a killer, or go to his room and clean up.

As he gave it some thought, a slightly built man with dark, close-set eyes and a thin, bloodless line for a mouth entered by the rear door. He wore a smooth-handled, well-oiled pistol low on his hip. The holster was thonged to his thigh with rawhide string which caused it to tip forward, holding the butt of the weapon it pocketed at the favored, quickly-grasped angle preferred by professional gunmen. Starbuck wondered who he might be.

The bartender answered the question for him. "The usual, Mr. Ruch—rye?"

This was the party Gentry had asked about, Shawn realized as he watched the gunman take up the shot-glass the bartender had set before him and follow Gentry to one of the tables. At once the aproned man behind the counter swung to Starbuck.

"Ready for that refill?"

Shawn shook his head, draining the glass. "One'll hold me for a spell. Sheriff's office here close?"

The bartender lifted the mug, rubbed at the circle of moisture it had left on the counter. "Sure is, Mister—Mister—"

"Starbuck. Don't bother with the mister."

"Habit of mine," the barkeep grinned. "Sheriff's office is down the street, and across. Ain't in town, however. Gone east for a visit with his folks. You got yourself some trouble?"

"Looking for a job—"

"Job? Well, Dave Englund's the deputy. See him, but I

don't know's he can do you much good—him already holding down the job."

"Not looking for a deputy job. I'm a ranch hand."

"I see," the bartender said and cast a thoughtful look at Gentry and Ruch. Whatever it was he had in mind passed, and he added: "Talk to Dave . . . expect he'll be able to help."

"Looking for somebody here, too—or information on him. My brother. You been in town long?"

"About three months. Just bought the place. . . . When was your brother here?"

"Not real sure he ever was, but it'd be a year or better."

"Let's me out, I reckon."

"Seems. Well, obliged to you. I'll go have a talk with the deputy right away."

"Sure thing, Mr. Starbuck. . . . Appreciate your trade."

Shawn grinned. When he returned to the lobby he took up his gear, and under the watchful eyes of the clerk, mounted the stairs to the balcony, off which turned a hallway leading to the rooms, some with numbers, others bearing the names of women.

He located number eight, unloaded his tack, and delaying only long enough to wash his face and hands, since he planned to treat himself to a tin-tub bath at the barbershop later. Returning to the street, he scanned the storefronts, located the lawman's quarters, and made his way to them.

An elderly man glanced up from the desk where he sat thumbing through the yellowed pages of a magazine as Shawn entered. He appeared to be the sole occupant in the heat-stuffed building.

"Yeh?"

"You Dave Englund?"

The older man snorted. "Ain't likely to be. I'm Kitch, the jailer. Deputy's out. Something I can do for you?"

Shawn noted a sudden, fixed interest on the jailer's part in his belt buckle. Kitch seemed to be taking in each minute detail of the scrolled, silver oblong.

"Could be. Looking for work. Thought maybe you'd know of some rancher needing a hand. Wrong time of the year, but I still need a job."

Kitch seemed to recover himself. He straightened, then frowned. "Well, man can probably hire on at Three Cross. Jim Kelso owns the outfit. Hear he needs hands."

Starbuck said, "Fine. . . . How do I get to his place?" He was thinking of the older man's interest in the buckle, wondering if it had deeper meaning—something more than simple curiosity. It would pay to question him.

"Not far from here, ten mile more or less. . . . Where you staying?"

"The Amador."

"Well, just come out the front door, turn right 'til you cross the river, then head south. Misdoubt, however, there's any powerful hurry. Jobs at Three Cross are mighty plentiful."

"Meaning what?"

"Well, things've been happening out there, and the way it's going for him—say, that's him coming now. . . . Can save yourself a ride and do your asking right here."

Starbuck stepped to the doorway, smiling at his good fortune. He wasn't too enthusiastic about taking on an additional twenty miles in the saddle for the day unless it was absolutely necessary. Moving out onto the landing, he prepared to hail the rancher. Kelso was pulling in to the hitchrack that fronted the sheriff's office.

= 4 =

Kelso, a harried, bleak man with shadowed eyes and graying hair, swung down stiffly from the tall bay he was riding. Spinning the tag ends of the reins about the cross bar of the rack, he strode into the sheriff's office. Glancing about, he halted in the center of the stuffy room.

"Where's the deputy?"

Kitch said, "Out—ain't sure where. Something I can do for you?"

"There's a plenty the law can do," the rancher said wearily. "When'll Morrison be back?"

"Week, maybe ten days. Unless he changes his mind and stays longer. . . . More trouble at your place?"

"Never quits. Another line shack was burned down two nights ago. . . . Now, about two dozen of my steers've been slaughtered."

"Slaughtered?"

"What I said. Bastards run them down into an arroyo, shot them through the head, left them piled up there."

Kitch wagged his head dolefully. "A hell of a thing. I'll tell Dave about it. All I can do."

"Not all he can do, by God! I want the law moving in on this! Something's got to be done about all this hell-raising. Nobody else's having any trouble but me—and that must mean something. Totes up now to where I've had three line shacks burned to the ground—and have lost close to a hundred head of beef, one way or another. It's got to be stopped—hear?"

"Sure, Mr. Kelso, but—"

"You tell the deputy everything I've said—and you make sure he's listening." Abruptly the rancher pivoted on his heel, started for the door.

Shawn, ignored throughout the conversation, took a step forward. "Kelso—"

The cattleman paused, looked impatiently over his shoulder. "Yeh?"

"Name's Starbuck. Just rode in from Arizona. I'm looking for a job—cowhand. Was told you might be wanting a man."

"Wanting!" the rancher echoed bitterly. "That's the

24

wrong word—needing's more like it." He cocked his head to one side, squinted at Shawn. "You know what's going on at my place?"

"Only what I heard you telling the jailer. Just came in, like I mentioned."

Kelso's eyes narrowed, filled with suspicion. "That the truth—that you just got here?"

Shawn's temper lifted. "The truth," he said stiffly. "Why the hell would I lie about it?"

He could have added that he'd been west of the settlement earlier, involved in preventing a stagecoach holdup— a fact the driver, Henry Mason, and the guard, George Eberhardt, could verify, but the stubbornness in him would not permit it; either Kelso took his word, or he didn't.

"No offense," the rancher said, no apology in his tone. "Hired help's one of my problems—and I'm mighty sick of the way I'm being treated. Can't get a man to stay with me more'n a few days. Some come to me and tell me they've got a job somewheres else. Others just pull out and I never see them again. I get the feeling they hired on just long enough to do some damage—or they're scared off."

"Scared off—by who?" Kitch asked in a voice that made it plain it was an old question often asked. "You've never give us nothing to work on. You tell us who to go after and we'll do it—like the sheriff's always saying."

"How the hell can I tell you who it is when I don't know myself? Ought to be the law's job, stepping in, finding out who and what's at the bottom of the burnings and poisonings and killing off of my stock—"

"Ain't nothing we can do unless we've got something to go on. The sheriff—"

"Sounds like you've got more than your share of problems," Starbuck cut in, realizing that he was once again about to get involved in another man's trouble. . . . But he needed the work—and jobs were scarce.

"My share and then some," Kelso said. He studied Shawn for a long moment. "Reckon that means you ain't asking for the job now."

Starbuck's shoulders moved slightly. "You're looking to hire a hand, I'm needing work. It's that simple. Got to admit, however, my belly's about full of taking on somebody else's grief."

The rancher nodded. "Something I can easy savvy, and I don't blame you. No sense hunting trouble. Comes to a man without him half looking for it. . . . Reckon any man

25

with a lick of sense would never sign on at Three Cross—not the way things are going."

"Didn't say I was turning down the offer, just said I was tired of being in the middle."

Kelso brushed his hat to the back of his head. "That mean you're hiring on?"

"Up to you."

The rancher stared at Shawn, grinned, bobbed in pleased agreement. "All right, you're working for me—and I've got me a hunch you ain't the kind I've been having to put up with. . . . You're on as a regular hand."

"Suits me. Got my gear and horse at the Amador. Give me a few minutes to go pick them up, then I'm ready."

"Nothing wrong with me going with you," Kelso said briskly. "Could stand a drink. Then we can ride out together."

The rancher moved toward the door. Starbuck, nodding to the jailer, followed. Together they crossed to the rack where Kelso freed his horse. Shoulder to shoulder in the afternoon's bright heat, they walked to the hotel.

Shawn, summoning the same boy who had met him on arrival, ordered the chestnut saddled and brought up. As both men entered the Spanish Dagger by its rear entrance and stepped up to the bar, the man behind the polished counter greeted them cheerfully.

"Mr. Kelso—good to see you again! And Mr. Starbuck! Let's see—it'll be whiskey and a beer, as I recollect."

"Right, Arnie," the rancher replied with no particular show of friendliness. He lifted his brows to Shawn. "Beer all you drink?"

"Make it a whiskey this time," Starbuck said, and added to Kelso: "While it's coming I'll run upstairs and get my stuff."

On his return he halted at the desk. "Got myself a job so I won't be needing the room. What do I owe you for washing up?"

The clerk frowned painfully. "Four bits'll cover it," he said tiredly, and hung the key back on its proper hook.

Starbuck paid off, retraced his steps to the bar, noting as he crossed from the archway that the gunman, Vern Ruch, and the military-like Gentry were still at the same table. His drink was waiting for him on the counter, and stepping up beside Kelso, saddlebags draped over one shoulder, he propped his rifle against his legs and wrapped his fingers around the glass.

"*Salud!*" the rancher said in a hopeful voice as he lifted his whiskey. "Here's to better days."

26

Shawn nodded, said, "Luck," and downed the fiery liquor.

Kelso drew a coin from his vest pocket, looked expectantly at Shawn. "Another?"

"One does me good—two's too many," Starbuck said. "Go ahead if it suits you. I'm sure in no hurry."

The cattleman shrugged. "Enough," he said and came about. His glance touched Gentry and the gunman. "Howdy," he murmured, and moved on toward the door.

Outside they found the young Mexican waiting with the chestnut. Shawn dropped a dollar—one of his last—in his hand to pay for the gelding's care, slid the rifle into its boot, and slinging the saddlebags across the skirt of the hull, stepped up. Kelso was settled and waiting.

"Place's not far from here—ten miles, about. Got to ford the river, head south. ... Ride'll work up an appetite."

Jim Kelso seemed in better spirits. The drink probably, Starbuck thought as they pulled away from the rack. Abruptly his head came up as his eyes caught the figures of two men entering the Golden Horseshoe at the upper end of the street. He had only a fleeting glimpse of the pair but there was no doubt in his mind as to their identity—the two outlaws who had escaped during the attempted holdup of the west-bound stage—Dallman and the Kid.

Deputy Dave Englund, his red hair plastered to his skull with sweat, alkali dust loading his stubble of beard, thrust his face into the pan of water he'd poured from the prisoner's bucket and scrubbed vigorously. Then, snorting and blowing appreciatively, he straightened up. Grabbing the towel that hung above the basin at the rear of the jail, he swiped at his dripping features, slanting a look at Bud Kitch. "It's hotter'n hell caved in out there," he said, and then added: "Now, tell me again."

The old jailer swore irritably, moved to the doorway, and spat into the powdery dust beyond the stoop. "Goddangit, pay attention this time!"

"Was paying attention—just trying to get it straight."

Kitch looked up and down the street, near deserted at that supper hour, spat again. "Which you needing to get straight—what Kelso said or what I said about this here Starbuck?"

"Hell with Kelso. He knows there ain't nothing I can do for him. It's Starbuck I'm interested in."

"Like I said, it come to me first off when he come

27

walking in here that he was the killer Morrison's been looking for."

Englund paused, digging the towel into his ears as he studied the floor. "Don't make sense. ... Was it him, why would he show up here? Be natural for him to stay as far away from this town as he could, not come sashaying right into the sheriff's office."

"Not 'specially. Got to remember that jasper he tangled with didn't die right off. Was several days—and he'd already pulled out by then. ... Dave, I'm telling you for sure, he's the one!"

Englund hung the towel on its peg, swore. "Too goddam bad there ain't at least one picture of him a man could go by—"

"I don't need one. Know you never seen this Friend, but I have, and Morrison has. Starbuck's a mite taller and skinnier looking, but he could've lost some weight. That'd make him seem taller."

"Guess it would at that."

"And he's one of them boxers. Wears a real fancy belt buckle with some kind of a carving on it—a man standing there in them long drawers and a sash around his middle with his fists held up like they do—"

"Could've bought the buckle, or maybe stole it, or won it in a poker game—"

"Sure," Kitch said in disgust. "Moon's made of green cheese, too."

The deputy grinned at the older man, checked his chin in the cracked mirror above the basin. ... The hell with it, he'd wait until morning to shave.

"Now, don't get all het up," he said. "Just trying to find all the holes in what you're saying—and thinking. You know how Morrison is."

Kitch turned back into the sweltering room. "Then you're agreeing?"

"Only saying you're maybe right. A lot of it sure fits. Biggest thing that don't is why he'd come back here. Had trouble once in this town, what'd bring him back?"

The old jailer was silent for a time. Finally he raised his head, nodded thoughtfully. "Yeh, why? Now, that's got me to wondering, too. Him coming here to 'Cruces, saying he needed a job—and just happening to be handy when Jim Kelso rode in."

"Exactly. He could maybe be mixed up in this trouble that keeps popping up at Three Cross."

"Does sort of look like a hired gun."

"And him jumping at the chance to go to work for Kelso . . . seems kind of funny."

Kitch shrugged. "Well, I ain't sure there's any hookup there, but I'll swear he's this jaybird Morrison's hunting. Be smart to haul him in, lock him up until the sheriff gets back and can have a look at him."

"Ought to have a reason first. He's probably a pretty smart one when it comes to the law—and all we've got to hold him on is a hunch. I can ask around town, see if anybody else recognized him."

"Wasn't hardly here long enough for that."

"Can ask, anyway. Besides, him hiring out to Kelso means he'll be around for a few days at least—unless he gets run off like the others."

"Misdoubt that. I don't figure him for the kind somebody's going to scare off."

"Maybe. . . . Could be he ain't supposed to get drove off," the deputy said, reaching for his hat. "Let me do some feeling around. . . . Things shape up right, I'll run down to El Paso, send a telegram to Morrison, ask him what we ought to do."

Kitch grunted in satisfaction, drew out his plug of black tobacco. "If you do, you can tell the sheriff for me that I'm willing to bet he's our man."

"Way it looks," Englund admitted, moving to the door, "I'd be a fool to take that bet. . . . Going to get myself a bite to eat. Be back in a hour or so. . . ."

5

Ignoring the bridge, Starbuck and Kelso forded the Rio Grande a half mile or so below town, and in the hard, whiskey-colored light of late afternoon, rode up onto a well-rutted wagon trail paralleling the river's west bank.

A hint of fall was in the air, and the light wind drifting in from the north carried a tang of woodsmoke and burning brush. The cottonwoods—great, spreading umbrellas with trunks six feet and more in diameter, that had furnished relief from the searing sun for the Spanish *conquistadores*, centuries earlier, as they marched up the valley in search of the fabled Seven Cities of Gold—were already tipping their leaves with flaming yellow.

As if to further the fashion in color, rabbit brush, the sunflowers, crownbeard along the marshy sinks, oddly round snakeweed, and even the tangled clumps of wicked, prickly pear cactus—all showed blossoms in varying shades of yellow. Only the asters were at contrariety, proclaiming their individuality with rich, purple faces.

Starbuck drank it all in as a man thirsting, never tiring of nature's flamboyant offerings, his wandering gaze missing nothing—a covey of blue quail scampering along a sandy arroyo, hurrying for the hills to their right; he saw the doves, noted they were gathering, preparing to wing their way south into Mexico for the winter months; he watched a lone jack rabbit spring from beneath the horse's hooves, bound off, his foot-tall, black-tipped ears starchily erect.

All seemed lost to Jim Kelso, however. Shawn slid a glance to the man from the corner of his eye, noticed the preoccupied grimness, the near-desperate manner of the rancher.

"Your brand—Three Cross—you take that from the name of the town?" he asked, hoping to break the rancher's silence.

Kelso shifted on his saddle. "No—from the land, or from a hill that's behind the house, actually. Found three crosses standing there, all sort of bunched together. Graves, I figured. Nobody seemed to know."

"Probably some of the folks heading for California and the gold rush—but didn't make it."

"Doubt it. Crosses had been there a long time. Not much left now—they were just wood. Daughter of mine, Julie, piled rocks where they were so's they wouldn't be lost. She said somebody meant for whoever it was to be remembered and she'd do her part by marking the spot."

"How long've you been ranching in this valley?"

Kelso brushed at the sweat on his face. "Most of ten years. Came west after the war. Found this place, liked it. Done right well—up until this trouble hit."

Starbuck nodded. "Was listening to you talk to the jailer. Sounds plenty bad. Usually a reason why a thing like this happens."

The rancher turned to Shawn. His eyes were dull, tired looking. "Reason—you think maybe I've done something to—"

"Not specially—just that whoever it is, is doing it for a purpose. . . . You have any trouble getting your land?"

"Trouble?"

"Yeh, like having to drive off squatters—something along that line."

Kelso shook his head. "Land was vacant—clear. Got near a hundred thousand acres, not all mine, of course; a lot of it is open range that I'm using. But I've never had to run off one solitary soul—not one. Was never anybody living on any part of it, the free or the deeded."

Starbuck mulled that about in silence as they rode steadily on, following now the crest of a long, running ridge that was beginning to slant toward the west. . . . There had to be some reason for the trouble plaguing Kelso's Three Cross ranch; things like wantonly slaughtered cattle, poisoned water holes, and burned down line shacks didn't just happen for no cause.

"There been anybody around wanting to buy you out?"

Kelso made an indifferent gesture with his hand. "Been a few over the years, as I recollect. Only one lately. That was several months back."

"Who?"

"Don't actually know. Banker drove up from El Paso one day and made me an offer. Was good enough but I didn't see no point in selling. Wife and daughter don't want to move—and what the hell would I do with myself if I wasn't raising cattle? So I turned him down."

"He get riled up over that?"

The rancher rubbed at the side of his neck where the sun was making itself felt. "Not so's I could notice. Blaisdell was making the offer for another man, not himself. All in a day's work to him, I expect . . . Why? You think maybe there's a connection?"

"Somebody who wanted your place real bad could be trying to force your hand."

Kelso shrugged. "Hell, that was months ago, and I've heard of Blaisdell. Big man in that part of Texas—well thought of. He'd not be mixed up in something like you're talking about."

"Might not know anything about what's going on. But if that was several months ago we can probably rule him and whoever he was working for out. . . . Your range run up close to the Mexican border?"

"No, stops quite a ways this side, in fact. Sort of had that idea myself once, that it could be *bandidos* coming across the line. Makes no sense, though. They'd maybe run off a few head of beef, steal everything in the shacks, but it wouldn't be like them to kill off a bunch of steers and let them lay."

"Expect you're right," Starbuck agreed. But the fact, lodged firmly in his mind, remained; there had to be a reason for all the trouble besetting Kelso.

"That belt you're sporting," the rancher said, pointing. "Buckle's mighty fancy. It mean something special?"

"Belonged to my pa. He was a boxer," Shawn replied. He'd gone through the explanation countless times, had often considered not wearing it just to avoid the need for the telling of its history, but he knew that would be a mistake. It was a magic key that opened many conversational doors and prepared the way for inquiries concerning Ben.

"Must've been a champion. . . . That's silver and real ivory, ain't it?"

Shawn nodded, went into the explanation, and then concluded: "Pa's dead now, and I'm trying to clear up the estate. Reason I'm in this country. I'm looking for my brother, Ben. Left home about ten years ago."

The cattleman's brows lifted. "You figure he's around here?"

"Could be—and he's just as apt to be working cattle in Canada or growing wheat in Nebraska. Could be dead. There's nothing for sure and all I can do is what I've been doing now for quite a spell—hunt for him."

"Oughtn't be too hard. Name like Starbuck's not the commonest."

"Probably goes by something else. Swore he'd never use the family name again when he ran off. . . . Sort of got the idea he was around Las Cruces for a time. Would probably have put on a boxing show. You remember anything like that? Would've been a year or so ago."

Kelso thought for a long minute, finally said: "Seems I recollect something about a fancy boxer being in town, but I ain't for certain. Never saw him myself, do know that. Fact is, I don't go into town much. Leave it to my womenfolk and the hired help to do the trotting back and forth. . . . Sorry I ain't much help."

Starbuck sighed heavily. "Just a hunch, anyway. Something comes to your mind later I'll be obliged if you'll mention it."

"Can bet I will. Ten years is a long time, however. You couldn't't've been much more'n a button when this—this—"

"Ben—"

"This Ben run off. How do you expect to recognize him if you ever do come face to face?"

"Has a scar over his left eye. Only certain thing I can depend on."

They fell silent after that as the road swung down into a fairly deep arroyo. Large rocks and thick stands of Apache plume, with occasional clumps of mesquite hemmed the twin ruts on either side, and here and there a tall, grotesque agave thrust itself high above the shorter growth as if anxious to feel the first sun's rays in the morning and their last, lingering touch at night.

"Saw you speak to a couple of men in the saloon. Gentry and Ruch, the bartender called them. One called Ruch looked familiar."

Kelso shrugged. "He's a fancy gun-hawk from over Texas way. Don't know what Gentry's got him hanging around for. Man like Vern Ruch just naturally draws trouble."

Shawn agreed. There was always someone, usually with just enough liquor in his belly to fortify his courage, who would call out such a man as Ruch and promptly get himself shot to death for his pains. . . . The Ruchs of the world were bloodless machines, geared to one thing— ruthless, cold murder.

"What's Gentry do? Carries himself like he might've been in the war."

"Seems I heard somewheres he was an officer of some kind. Don't know much else. Been around 'Cruces for a time. Lives at the hotel. Seems to have money. Somebody said he was a buyer."

"Cattle?"

"Could be. Never once talked to me about my herd, though. Always figured—"

Jim Kelso's words were lost in a sudden hammering of pistols coming from the higher ridge to their right. The rancher cursed wildly as a bullet cut into his arm. He swore again as another slammed into the horse he was riding with a meaty sound, and sent the animal plunging headlong to the ground.

"The rocks!" Starbuck yelled, throwing himself off the chestnut. "They've got us cold here in the open!"

≡ 6 ≡

Starbuck hit the ground flat-footed, the impact jarring him solidly. A bullet whipped at him. He spun instantly, lunged for the shelter of a massive boulder a wagon bed length away. He saw Kelso as he whirled, realized for the first time that the rancher was wounded. He'd thought the horse was the only casualty.

Doubling back, and crouched low, he hurried to where the dazed Kelso was struggling to rise. Throwing an arm around the cattleman, Shawn lifted him bodily off the ground, and turning, dashed for the protection of the rock as lead spanged angrily from its weathered surface.

Heaving for breath, he propped the man against the thick segment of granite and said, "You hurt bad?"

He put the question to the rancher more as a matter of course than in the sense of needed information, since he was already pulling aside the bloodied sleeve to get at the wound.

"Not sure," Kelso murmured, frowning into Starbuck's sweating face. It was as if he were uncertain as to what had occurred.

"Was close—plenty close," Shawn said.

The rancher jerked involuntarily. "Goddammit to hell! What's happening to me?" he cried suddenly in a desperate, baffled voice.

Starbuck shook his head, paying little thought to the frantic words. He had cleared away the fabric of the rancher's shirt, and by pressing with his thumb, had checked the steady flow of blood in the furrow the bullet had gouged from the flesh. It wasn't a serious wound if treated properly, and soon. He looked closely into the man's eyes; the dazed wonderment had vanished and now there was only a dull, hopeless sort of defeat. By that he knew Kelso's senses had returned to normal.

"Press down here," he directed, and taking the rancher's fingers into his own, placed the thumb at the essential point. "Got to keep the bleeding stopped while I find something for a bandage."

Kelso bobbed his head, pointed to his downed horse by jutting his chin. "In my saddlebags—some clean rags."

Starbuck, on all fours, made his way along the side of the boulder to its front and paused. The shooting from above had ceased when they ducked out of sight, but he knew the bushwhackers had not gone; they were simply waiting—patiently.

He glanced about seeking a route to the dead horse that would afford better cover. The animal lay near center of the road, fully in the open and thus exposed to the marksmen above. He doubted he'd have much luck reaching it, but keeping low, he edged away from the boulder. Instantly the arroyo echoed with gunshots. The sandy earth ahead of Shawn leaped and boiled as bullets drilled into it.

"Forget it," Kelso called tiredly. "I'll make out."

Starbuck wormed his way back to where the rancher was slumped. He again examined the wound. The continual pressure on the vein involved had all but stopped the blood flow, but the instant application was released, it surged forth anew. A bandage was the only answer; Kelso, already showing signs of extreme fatigue, would not stand the strain much longer.

Resorting to the bandanna about his neck, Shawn drew it free, snapped it sharply to dislodge as much dust as possible. Then taking up a small pebble he substituted it for Kelso's thumb and secured it in place with the folded cloth. The wound began to bleed the instant the rancher removed his hand, but as Starbuck cinched down with the bandanna, and the small stone pushed deep into the flesh, the flow once again ceased.

"Need to ease up on that now and then," Starbuck said, pulling back. "But it'll work until we can get you to the doc." Drawing his pistol, he checked the loads in the cylinder and glanced to the ridge above the arroyo. "Next thing is to get out of here."

Kelso stirred, reached for his own weapon. "Not alone, you ain't. Up to me to help—you're hardly working for me yet."

"Minute you put me on the payroll back in town, I started. Makes me a Three Cross man, and I take what comes with the job. ... Now, sit quiet. I'll circle around and try coming in behind those bushwhackers."

"My fight," the rancher protested weakly. "I ought to go along. ... Maybe if we can nail one of them, I'll find out what this is all about."

"Do my best to get one for you," Starbuck promised grimly. "But you stay put. Easier for me to go it alone."

Immediately he pivoted on a heel, and keeping low and

close to the base of the butte lifting above them, hurried along through the brush until he came to a narow ravine that broke the smooth face of the formation.

Halting there he studied the road, the place where Kelso was lying was easily marked by its position to the dead horse and the general look of the land. The ambushers would be almost directly above the horse. The bullets, he recalled, had come pouring down from straight overhead. . . . Therefore, he should be well below the marksmen at that point where the wash broke onto the flat.

Removing his spurs and hanging them on a stump, he began to climb the declivity, doing it as quietly as possible, steadying himself by clinging to the tough scrub oak growing from the sides of the storm-slashed gully, bracing himself whenever possible against jutting rocks. By the time he gained the top and could look onto the level, he was sucking deep for wind, and sweat clothed him from head to foot.

Sagging against the edge of the wash, he mopped the mist from his eyes and squinted into the pale glare. Two horses, tied well back from the rim of the bluff, were a quarter mile or so distant. The bushwhackers would be holed up about opposite, he reasoned.

Reaching down, he laid his hand on the butt of his pistol, assuring himself that it had not dislodged during the climb, and then heaved himself out of the ravine. He could have used a few more minutes' rest to ease the trembling muscles of his legs, unaccustomed to such strain, as well as to allow his breathing to subside to normal; but he felt he had little time to spare.

Kelso, while not wounded dangerously, should get medical attention as soon as possible. He was not a young man, and the injury, if neglected for an appreciable extent, could mean trouble. Dropping back a short distance from the lip of the butte, Starbuck, again bent low, moved hurriedly forward.

Motion off to his far left, just over the lip of the bluff dropped him flat on his belly. The stained, peaked crown of a hat bobbed into view along the rim, disappeared, showed once more. Starbuck clucked softly. Now he knew where the outlaws were hiding.

The hat vanished. Shawn raised himself, probed the near-flat surface of the butte. It offered no arroyos or depressions along which he could make an approach. He'd simply have to go straight in, depending a great deal on luck.

Pistol in hand he edged forward, doubly careful now to

stay below the lip of the butte and not allow himself to become silhouetted against the sky.

He halted abruptly. A man was standing upright just below the rim, staring at him in surprise. The rider reacted. His arm streaked down for the pistol at his side, came up in a blur of glinting metal. Starbuck dipped to one side, triggered the weapon in his hand. The explosions came together, slapping loudly, setting up a rolling chain of echoes.

The bushwhacker staggered back. His knees buckled as the pistol fell from his nerveless fingers. He took several stumbling steps and disappeared over the edge of the butte.

Shawn, muscles taut, nerves keyed to smoothness, hunched low, waiting for the second man to make his move. Jim Kelso was going to get his wish. He had a dead man to see, and from him perhaps he would learn who it was that was trying to ruin him and Three Cross. . . . Whoever, they were playing for keeps—there was no doubt of that.

The minutes dragged by as the sun began to spread its last, steaming rays across the hills and flats before relinquishing dominion to night. . . . What the hell was holding back the other bushwhacker?

Starbuck squirmed in the uncomfortable heat, brushed at his eyes again. Suddenly out of patience, he moved on, working his way cautiously, attention riveted to the lip of the butte and the narrow slope just below it that extended, like a shelf, for a few feet before it broke off into a sheer drop.

Another storm wash appeared immediately ahead offering him an avenue by which he could get off the flat and down onto the bench. It would be a good move; there was ample rock and brush there to cover his movements. Sliding into the cut, he lowered himself to the bench. He should be able to locate the second outlaw now with no trouble.

Continuing, he made his way quietly along the shelf, placing each booted foot carefully, avoiding the loose shale, the swish of disturbed bushes, and crackle of dead brush as much as possible. He halted, swore deeply as the quick pound of a horse leaving fast reached him.

Lunging upright, he threw his glance to where the bushwhackers had picketed their horses. Only one remained. The other, ridden by a man in dark clothing and hunched low over the saddle, was racing off into the trees.

Shaking his head he stared after the man until he had

disappeared. He had hoped to be of real help to Kelso; a live prisoner could have been made to talk, answer a few questions. Turning, he climbed up onto the little mesa capping the butte and crossed to where the horse waited; a dead man couldn't speak but perhaps his identity would mean something.

The outlaw was a stranger to Jim Kelso—a man he'd never laid eyes on during all his years in the valley, he declared, when later, astride the dead man's horse, Shawn took him to view the body. Nor was there any identification in his pockets or among his gear that was of help. The buckskin he forked wore an unfamiliar brand.

"Just some drifter what hired out to whoever's doing this to me," Kelso said, and then as Starbuck started to hoist the body to the back of his saddle on the chestnut, he added: "Leave him be. I'll send one of the hands back with a wagon, have him toted into town. ... Maybe the deputy or somebody around there'll know him."

Shawn nodded, swung onto the gelding. The rancher appeared weak and evidently was experiencing considerable pain. He needed to be in the hands of a doctor.

"We far from your place?"

"Less'n an hour," Kelso replied, and then wagged his head. "Ain't no sense going back to town, if that's what you're thinking. Myra—my wife—can do a better job of patching up a man than any doc—seven days a week! Living out like we've done all our lives, we learned to make do and get by. ... Anyways, been hurt worse than this many a time."

Starbuck nodded. If Three Cross was that near it would be wiser to continue. Wheeling the chestnut about, he aimed for the road, Kelso following silently while a deep frown pulled at his lean features.

"Obliged to you for stepping in the way you did," he said.

"Why not? Was part of the job, far as I'm concerned."

"Not the way most of them I've been hiring would look at it. ... Can see how you're built. ..." Kelso's words faded as the horses began to pull up out of the arroyo for the flat above. He was clinging to the saddle horn with one hand, and clamped the other over his wound. There was a translucent look to his features.

"Would like to think," he continued, when the pain from the sharp jolting had ended, and they were on the level, "that you'd stick with me a spell—as my *caporal*—foreman, I expect they call it where you come from."

Starbuck glanced at the rancher in surprise. "I appreciate the offer, but I doubt if it would set well with your other men. Probably some of them've been with you a long time and have earned the job."

"All too old for it. They know it, same as I do. Be no grumbling on that score. Fact is, I've hired on three *caporals* in about as many months—and all quit me. Pay'll be good. Ninety a month and found—and I'll sure not butt into your way of ramrodding things."

"Not meaning to argue, but you hardly know me—"

"Learned all I need to know about you back there in the canyon. Ain't hard to gauge a man once you've seen him standing up to trouble."

"Something else—I'm not the kind to stay long in one place. Got to keep moving on, looking for Ben."

"Well, that's your business but, far as your brother's concerned, my advice is to forget him, settle down before you waste your life away."

"Probably good advice," Starbuck said slowly, "only I can't take it. Ben's got to be found."

"It's that important to you, eh?"

"It is. . . . But if it'll help some I'll take over, work for you until the first of the year. Came here figuring to find a job for that long. Then I'll be moving on."

Kelso sighed wearily. "All right—reckon a while's better'n nothing. I'll nod you off to the crew, such as I've got, tell them you're the new boss. . . . Anything special you want them told—or don't?"

"Can't think of anything. Something comes up, I'll do my own talking."

Shawn looked ahead into a shallow, green basin in which stood, in quiet serenity, a collection of neat buildings, spreading trees, and splashes of brightly colored flowers. A strip of silver marked the course of a small stream making its way across the swale, and near dead center a windmill wheeled lazily in the slow breeze. . . . This was Three Cross.

= 7 =

With the last of the sun turning the sky into a golden dome, Starbuck and Jim Kelso rode into the yard. Immediately two women burst from the back door of the long adobe and wood ranch house, and came hurrying up anxiously. Kelso's wife and daughter, he assumed, allowing his eyes to run over the orderly place with its well-kept corrals and structures.

A fine place, he thought, and wondered as he had so many times, if the day would ever come when he could stop, have a home such as this; and as before the answer was the same—first find Ben.

"Now, don't fuss over me!" Kelso's complaining voice broke into his consciousness. "Ain't hurt bad, only nicked deep."

An elderly Mexican wearing a cook's apron had appeared at the door of a smaller building near the main house. A second man, also well in years, was trotting up stiffly from what evidently was the crew's quarters, his seamy face grim. . . . It was a fine place, Starbuck decided again, but tension lay across it, a breathless sort of restraint that was almost tangible. It was as if the trees, the corrals, the buildings—Three Cross itself were waiting, wondering what would befall it next.

Shawn left the saddle, listening to the cattleman make his explanations to all within range, unconsciously giving the girl closer study. Julie, Kelso had called her. She was probably about his own age, maybe a year younger. She had dark-brown hair with reddish lights that the sun brought out, and against the creamy tan of her face her wide set eyes were very blue. She had an attractive figure that even her man's style shirt and corduroy riding skirt failed to conceal.

Mrs. Kelso—Myra, he recalled her name, too—was an older edition of her daughter except there was a gentleness to her as she went calmly about examining the wound in her husband's arm, despite his objections.

"Want you all to meet Shawn Starbuck," the rancher said, finally pulling away. "Wasn't for him I'd not be here now."

41

Shawn was aware of the instantaneous hostility that sprang to life in Julie Kelso's attitude. She wasn't one to trust any man far, he reckoned, and supposed she had good reason.

"My missus, my daughter, Julie. ... And this here is Aaron Lambert, one of my best men—and best friends," Kelso said, pointing each out individually. "Cook over there by the shack is Candido Aragon—we call him Candy. . . . Been with me a lot of years, too." He paused, glanced about and added, "Seems there ain't nobody else around right now. You'll have to meet the rest of the crew later."

Starbuck had shaken hands with each. Mrs. Kelso appeared grateful, Lambert cordial, Aragon polite. But there was a distinct suspicion and mistrust in Julie's manner.

"That's the *caporal's* quarters there next to the bunkhouse," Kelso said as he turned away with the two women at his sides. "Aaron, be obliged if you'll see Starbuck settled, get him what he needs. ... And tell Felipe to hitch up the wagon. There's a dead man lying out in Coyote Canyon. Have him hauled in to town and turned over to Dave Englund. Want to find out who he is. ... Maybe the law can do that much for me."

The old puncher bobbed his head, said, "Sure, Jim. Tend to it right away," and gathering up the reins of the two horses, beckoned to Shawn and moved off toward the barn.

Features sober, Lambert turning his watery eyes on Starbuck said, "mind telling me what happened out there? Didn't like pressing it in front of Jim's womenfolks."

"Ambush," Shawn replied. "Two men hiding on the bluff. Cut down on us when we rode through. One of them got away."

"That's it, then," Lambert muttered. "First blood's been drawed. Wonder what'll come next."

"Something make you think this is the start of bigger trouble?"

"Well, sure ain't never been nobody shot before, only cows. . . . You get a look at that bird who got away?"

"Too far off."

The older man swore. "Way it's been. Like a bunch of ghosts. Something always happening but nobody ever sees anything."

He'd be expected to change that, put a stop to all such problems, Starbuck realized, halting in front of the small cabin designated as his living quarters.

Stepping up to the chestnut, he pulled off his saddlebags

and drew his rifle, laying them on the small, square stoop that fronted the door. Then untying the strings, he removed his blanket roll.

"From what Kelso said you're one of the long-time hands."

Lambert hawked, spat. "Longest. Been here longer'n anybody 'cepting maybe old Candy."

Shawn picked up his belongings, pushed the door open. "Later I'd like talking to you. Few things I'd appreciate knowing."

"Sure enough. Can be back soon's I get these horses in the barn and start Felipe out with that wagon."

"I'll be inside," Shawn said, and stepped into the single room.

Its most recent occupant apparently had not been gone for long, he guessed, tossing the blanket roll onto a bench. Propping the rifle against a wall, he hung the saddlebags over the foot of the bed, sat down, tried out the mattress. It was hard, crackled noisily, and the springs protested his every move, but it would do. The way things were shaping up he'd likely spend damned few hours on it, anyway.

Rising, he unbuckled the straps of the leather pouches and began to distribute his belongings. He'd learned to travel light, accumulate nothing other than the actual necessities such as razor, soap, towel, a change of clothing, and extra ammunition for his weapons. A man on the move was foolish to load himself down with—

The rap of quick, firm footsteps on the landing brought him around to the doorway. The screen jerked back and Julie Kelso, features taut, stood in the rectangle of half light.

Shawn swept her with a calculating glance, assessed her manner. Here was trouble—a problem. He nodded coolly. "Something gone wrong with your pa?" he asked, getting in the first word.

She shook her head irritably. He could see the anger in her and it at once stirred temper within him. What the hell was eating her? He wasn't responsible for what was happening on Three Cross—or for her pa getting shot. He was just one of the hired hands.

Pulling off the new hat he'd bought in Lynchburg, just before beginning the journey, he tossed it onto the dusty table, folded his arms and waited. ... It was Julie Kelso who had something sticking in her craw—therefore it was up to her to open the ball.

She looked him up and down, inventoried his scant

43

possessions with a sweeping glance, and said, "You don't seem much like the others."

The words meant nothing to Shawn. He shrugged. "So?"

"You don't fool me any. Maybe you can the rest, but I see you for what you are—another of the bunch that's out to ruin us. Expect you had that ambush all arranged so's you could put yourself in good with my father."

"Sure did," Starbuck drawled. "Was so anxious that I plugged one of my own pals—the one that wagon's going out after right now," he added, pointing into the yard.

"That could have been a slip-up—your shooting him," Julie said, flatly dismissing the point. "I notice you didn't get hurt."

"Was born lucky, I reckon. . . . Anything else on your mind?"

"Plenty, Mister Starbuck! Like I said you may have fooled my father but not me. I figure you're just another of the bunch that's causing us trouble, and as soon as you do what you've been sent to do, you'll pull out like all the others who've hired on for a few days—"

"Pull out?"

"You know what I mean! Every rider we've put to work in the last three or four months just up and left."

"Not what I'm figuring to do."

"Expected you to say that—but I want you to know one thing sure," the girl rushed on ignoring his words, "maybe you're the *caporal,* but I'm keeping my eye on you—on just you every minute I can. . . . I see you make one wrong move and I'm going to put a rifle bullet in you! That clear?"

"Clear," Shawn echoed mildly. "Anything else?"

Julie stared at him. She was furious, beside herself, and her eyes were snapping. "Don't you laugh at me—I mean every word I say! I'm not easily fooled like my father—and I don't have a soft heart like him either!"

Shawn was tempted to say: *you're a hell of a lot prettier, too,* but he checked the words. Julie Kelso was in deadly earnest, worried to the peak of distraction. It would be cruel to show he did not take her seriously. . . . But his own nerves were a little on the raw side and he was laboring to keep his temper under control.

"Make you a deal," he said slowly. "You go right ahead keeping an eye on me. I won't mind that a bit—just as long as you don't get in the way of me doing a job for your pa."

44

"For my pa—father!" she scoffed. "For your boss, whoever he is, you mean!"

"For your pa," Starbuck repeated coldly. He was tired, sweaty, hungry, and his patience was rapidly running out. "Now, we've both had our say. You don't like me and I've got you figured for a nuisance. That's settled. I'll be obliged if you'll get out of here, let me clean up—that is unless you want to stick around and watch me strip off naked."

Reaching up he freed the buttons of his shield shirt, pulled it over his head, baring a bronzed, muscular torso. At once the girl spun, hastened for the door.

"If I—"

"If you've got anything more to say," Starbuck supplied, "best you tell it to your pa. He's the man who hired me. He'll have to be the one who fires me."

Abruptly Julie bolted through the doorway and into the yard. Shawn stood motionless, listening to the quick beat of her heels as she crossed the hardpack, and then turned again to the bed, resuming the interrupted chore of laying out his gear. He paused again, wearily, as a noise drew his attention. Harsh words rose to his lips. If it was Julie coming back—

It wasn't the girl but Aaron Lambert. "It all right if I come in?" the old puncher asked, and entered without waiting for Starbuck's answer.

Shawn grinned. "Sure. Find yourself a chair and get comfortable. Need to hear a few things about this place."

"Fire away," Lambert said, sitting down. "First off, howsomever, want to put in a word for the little gal. Just seen her go flying across the yard, tail feathers stiff, and head up like the heel flies was after her. Don't you feel too mean towards her. She's fretting plenty about her pa and about what's happening around here."

"Not hard to see that."

"Now, I don't exactly know how I ought to say this, but Jim's sort of easy going and nice like. He just don't quite seem to savvy how to buck up against things and straighten them out—if you get what I'm saying. ... Was she running the place, you can bet thing's would be different."

"She's given me a sample of what she'd do—or like to. Got the idea she not only doesn't trust me half as far as she could throw Durham bull, but unless I comb my hair the way she likes, I'm liable to wake up with a 44-40 bullet in my head."

"That's her all right," Lambert chuckled, and then sobered. "But don't poke no fun at her, son. She ain't

45

deserving of it. Shouldering a powerful big load, that girl, and soon's she finds out you're on the square, she'll be all for you." The old rider paused, looked directly into Starbuck's eyes. "You are, ain't you?"

The bluntness of the question, the direct and simple honesty of it hit Starbuck hard. He nodded soberly, took a step nearer the oldster and extended his hand.

"I am," he said, enclosing Lambert's gnarled fingers in his own. "That's my guarantee. I aim to give Jim Kelso the best that's in me. Goes for everybody and everything on Three Cross. Now, what I want to know is, who's out to kill him?"

=== 8 ===

The old rider stared thoughtfully at the warped toes of his scuffed, worn boots. After a time he reached into his pocket and drew forth a charred briar pipe. Knocking the dottle into the palm of his hand, he leaned forward, tossed the crumbs into a wood box beside the small White Oak heating stove, and settled back.

"I purely don't know—and that's a fact," he said, digging out a muslin sack of twist tobacco. Pinching off a quantity, he deliberately crushed the shards into fine bits, and stuffed them into the blackened bowl. "Same as I just can't figure why anybody'd be so all fired sot on ruining him."

"What about people who don't like him—other ranchers, maybe, or somebody in town."

"Jim's always been a good friend to folks. I can't think of nobody that'd be hating him."

Starbuck shrugged. "He's got an enemy somewhere, which is about normal, I suspect. Never met a man who didn't have."

"Sort of goes with being alive—like breathing and eating and such," Lambert agreed.

Shawn had asked the question of Kelso himself, now he asked it of the man's best and oldest friend. "There somebody wanting to buy Three Cross?"

The old puncher considered the thin stream of smoke snaking upwards from his pipe. "Recollect there was this lawyer from El Paso. He come up here, made an offer for some friend of his'n. Jim told him he wasn't interested and that was the end of it, far as I know."

"How long ago was that?"

Lambert sucked at his lower lip. "Let's see, this here's September. Was two, three months back—July, that's when it was. We'd just sold off a big chunk of the herd."

The offer to buy had been made more recently than Kelso had led him to believe—at least that was the impression he'd gotten. The rancher, however, had taken the offer lightly; it could be that the time had not registered definitely in his mind.

"How big a herd you running?" Shawn asked, moving

47

to the sink in the corner of the room and levering a pan of water from the pump.

"Somewheres close to two thousand head. Sold off better'n twenty-five hundred this summer. Market was plenty high and Jim grabbed the chance to clean up."

Starbuck washed himself thoroughly and toweled off; that complete bath he'd been looking forward to would still have to wait, however. There were a few things that needed doing first.

"From what I gathered from talking to Kelso and listening to his daughter, you're having no luck keeping hired help."

"Ain't no big mystery to it. They get scared off. All these goings on—fires and shootings and the like, it sure brings the yellow out in some, but maybe you can't fault them. Ain't no man in his right mind going to like bucking for the graveyard. ... Been a few who didn't even wait to collect their wages."

"Any of them ever actually get hurt?"

"Was some who claim they was shot at, but there weren't none that ever got hit. Jim's the first, like I told you. Had one fellow who got hisself caught in a little stampede."

"Stampede?"

"Yeh. Herd had been split into a couple a dozen bunches. Somebody or something set a jag to running. Puncher name of Gillespie got sort of trapped in front of them when his horse stepped in a gopher hole and throwed him. He got out of the way by jumping behind a mesquite. Wasn't hurt none, but it put the frost into him good. Quit that same day. Said he knew for certain somebody'd started them critters to running, done it just to get him tromped on."

Shawn, pulling on a clean if badly wrinkled shirt, walked to the doorway, looked out into the yard. The hill beyond the structures, mentioned by Kelso, was a round-topped bubble of lava rock covered with a thin grass. It appeared deceptively smooth in the faint light.

The ground at the foot of the formation was in shadow, but complete darkness was creeping up swiftly, swallowing all in its path as it swept skyward. He could not see the mounds where the crosses had stood, and had a quick wonder as to who might lie buried beneath them: simple peasants? adventuresome soldiers? Spanish noblemen in crested armor?

Shawn's interest sharpened. A horse and rider had appeared, and were now outlined on the crest of the hill.

"Somebody up on the *malpais*" he said, beckoning to Lambert.

The older man got to his feet, shuffled to the door. He squinted at the solitary figure for a long minute, shook his head.

"Ain't sure but it looks like that there *vaquero* we've seen hanging around now and then."

"Who is he?"

"Ain't nobody seems to know."

"Little strange, somebody like that just hanging around."

"Maybe not. We're close to the border and these *vaqueros* are funny birds. Work when they want, loaf when they take the notion. Independent as a hoot owl in a hollow log." Lambert looked up, glanced toward the corrals. "You want to meet the rest of the boys? They're coming in—leastways them that's been out with the herd. . . . Night crew's done rode off."

Shawn pulled on his hat. "Like to meet whoever's here now. Figure to ride out and say howdy to the others after I eat."

Stepping into the open, he glanced to the *malpais*. The rider had vanished. Tomorrow he'd do some scouting, see if he could encounter the man, and find out just why he was on Three Cross range. No drifter would stall around the same locality for any length of time without reason.

"Happened again—"

He swung to Lambert. The old puncher's gaze was on two men dismounting at the rack fronting the barn.

"What's that?"

"Them last hands Jim put to work—about a week ago. Two jaspers that blew in from over Texas way. They ain't with the others. Means they've pulled out."

"Maybe got busy—hung up—"

"Doubt it. They wasn't that anxious to work. Would've come in with Pierce and Dodd. The four of them's been working day shift with Jim and me pitching in to help out now and then. . . . Dan, where's them other boys?"

Pierce, a small, wiry man with a limp, jerked at his cinch strap. "Skedaddled," he said disgustedly. "Took off around sundown. Said to tell the boss they was quitting."

Shawn crossed to where the pair were removing their gear. "Name's Starbuck. Kelso's put me on as foreman," he said, offering his hand. "Those two give you any special reason why they were leaving?"

Dodd, a lanky oldster with glittering, dark eyes and a

49

saddle-leather face, spat into the dust. "Same reason they all give—it ain't healthy around here."

"They been shot at or threatened by somebody?"

Pierce wagged his head, looked questioningly at Dodd who also gave a negative response. "Didn't say nothing about it if they did."

Shawn turned away, hesitated. "One thing more, either of you notice a *vaquero* on the range lately?"

Again the riders exchanged glances. Dodd said: "Sure. Reckon we've all spotted him, just sort of ambling along. Don't do nothing or even get close enough to talk to. Just hangs around, lonesome like."

Starbuck nodded, continued on with Lambert at his side. "Who's doing the nighthawking?"

"Rafe Tuttle, Pete Helm, and Isidro Ortiz—with me spelling them off once in a while. Was three others on the night crew, but they took off a couple of days ago."

"Not many riders to be looking after two thousand head of beef," Shawn commented. It appeared to him that matters might be drawing to a head on Three Cross—the attempt to ambush Jim Kelso, the abrupt departure of half the hired help, which stripped the crew down to only a few elderly, ineffectual if loyal members. Something must be done, and done quickly.

"Like to get myself a bite to eat," he said then, coming to a decision.

"Sure. . . . Candy'll have supper waiting. . . . Come on."

Shawn ate a hasty meal, returned to the yard, and made his way to the barn with Aaron Lambert tagging at his heels.

"Need something to ride," he said, halting at the doorway. "Chestnut of mine's had a long day and needs some rest."

"Fermin!" Lambert bellowed. "You in here?"

From the black depths of the building a young Mexican appeared.

"You want something, *senor?*"

"This here's the new boss—the *caporal*. Get him a horse—that big black'll do."

"My gear, there on the rail," Starbuck said, smiling at the boy and pointing to his saddle straddling the adzed log placed in the first stall for such purpose.

He turned back into the yard to wait. Lamps had been lit in the main house and he could see Myra Kelso moving about inside her kitchen preparing the evening meal. Once Julie passed across the window, but he saw no sign of Kelso himself; most likely his wife had him resting in bed.

50

"You got something special in mind to do?" Lambert asked.

Shawn nodded. "One thing—see if I can find out what's going on around here. Got a feeling the next time they set an ambush for Kelso, he might not be so lucky."

"Thinking that, too. You got yourself an idea?"

"Not yet. It's what I'll be hunting for." Hearing a sound at the barn's entrance, he stepped aside as Fermin led a tall, black gelding into the open.

"You want some company?"

Starbuck smiled at the old puncher and mounted. "Obliged to you, but I'll go alone. Work better that way. Expect you're needing rest, anyway."

Lambert bobbed his head. "Ain't going to deny that. Now, you have a care. The range ain't exactly safe around here no more—'specially at night."

"I'm figuring on that."

The oldster stared, murmured, "Reckon I savvy," and then added, "Like to say it's mighty good to have somebody calling the turn here on the ranch again. ... Good night."

"Good night," Starbuck answered, and rode off.

=== 9 ===

Moving into the pale night, Shawn let his mind dwell upon the words Aaron Lambert had spoken. The old puncher made it sound as if Jim Kelso was doing little to keep Three Cross alive, that the ranch was more or less floundering along on its own strength. Perhaps that was true: it could be Kelso was a man not accustomed to fighting, and found himself at a loss as to what should be done.

His thoughts drifted to other things—to the cattle and the fact that with trouble apparently lurking behind every bush, only three men were riding herd on two thousand head. That was a situation that needed correcting as fast as possible, otherwise Three Cross would find itself out of business in short order. More cowhands, of course, was the solution—and likely some were available in Las Cruces, or certainly in the larger settlements of Albuquerque to the north and El Paso, only forty miles or less to the south.

But the catch wasn't finding men—it was keeping them once hired. Evidently the word was out and spread wide that Three Cross wasn't a good place for a man to hang his hat—not if he wanted to remain among the living. ... And the only way that reputation could be erased was to remove the threat—the source of the trouble.

Shawn sighed, realizing how fully he had become enmeshed in another man's problems. All he had intended doing was come down into the lower Rio Grande Valley, or the Mesilla—as some people called it, and find himself an ordinary job by which he could rebuild his depleted finances while he made discreet inquiries concerning a man who might be his brother.

Now, within hours after he'd arrived, where did he stand? He was the foreman of a ranch that was hock-deep in adversity; somebody was taking pot shots at the owner, and he, himself, was suspected of being a double-crosser by the rancher's own daughter. Added to those items was the fact that he had a couple of thousand steers to look after, and not half enough hired hands to assist in the doing.

Someday—someday he was going to find it possible to start out from one point, ride to another without any interruption, do what he had planned to do, free from detours and side issues, and then if the lead on Ben that had taken him to that particular destination proved false, just ride on. . . . Someday—maybe.

The black was enjoying the steady run in the evening's coolness, apparently having been stabled for some time, and Shawn drew him in, wanting to have as good a look at Three Cross range as possible. He was some distance from the ranch house, he noted, and crossing a broad, undulating plain of silver that was bordered on the west by rugged hills, and on the east by a band of trees. The river would lie there—the Rio Grande.

Other small groves marked the land with shadowy patchwork, and just below him he caught the circular shine of a water hole. Likely there were several of those scattered about, spring fed or possibly filled by seeps from underground streams.

A rider loomed up suddenly to his left, and came out from behind a clump of brush. Starlight glinted off the pistol held ready in his hand.

"Friend," Shawn said, and pulled to a halt.

The puncher came forward cautiously. A scar tracing down the side of his face looked white and slick in the half dark.

"Friend—who? Don't recollect ever seeing you before, cowboy."

"Name's Starbuck. Kelso put me on as foreman today. Which one are you, Tuttle or Helms?"

The rider, his eyes running over the black in recognition, relaxed gently, slid his pistol back into its holster.

"I'm Rafe Tuttle. Heard Jim'd brung in a new ramrod. Cook told us. Looking for something?"

"For anything and everything. Figure the biggest job I've got is to find out who's causing all the hell around here, and put a stop to it. Got any suggestions?"

Tuttle drew up one leg, hooked it around his saddle horn, and methodically began to build himself a cigarette.

"That's the devil of it," he said in a tired voice. "Can't nobody figure what it's all about. Things're just a happening, crazy like."

Shawn studied the old puncher. "We both know there's a reason for it. I've dug into the easy ones, got no answers. Could use some help."

Tuttle lit his quirley, the flame of the cupped match

53

placing a yellow shine on his taut, lean features and accentuating the high cheek bones.

"Was I knowing something I'd a done spoke up," he said quietly. "Three Cross is home to me, and the Kelsos are the only family I got. Same goes for Lambert and Pete and a couple others. We'd be fools to mess in our own nest, specially at our age."

Shawn nodded. What Rafe said made sense. All the riders who had stuck by Kelso were elderly men, past their yen for drifting, thinking now of the quiet years, and the need for a warm place to sleep, and a table at which they could sit down regularly. He could figure all of them—Aaron Lambert, Tuttle, Helms, Dodd, and the one with the limp, Dan Pierce, would do nothing to wrong Kelso.

That left the cook, Candy, the stable boy, Fermin, and a couple more: the one Kelso had sent after the outlaw's body, Felipe, and a regular range hand, Isidro. The first two he could count out; they'd have neither reason nor opportunity to be involved. Felipe he'd have to see later. Isidro was with the herd.

Tuttle leaned forward, eyes on Starbuck. "You aiming to stay, or you like them others—just passing through?"

"I'll be here. I don't aim to pull out tomorrow or the next day—or the next. But I've got to straighten things out fast. The herd on ahead?"

Rafe bobbed his head. "In the east valley. Going to start them drifting towards the river in the morning."

Starbuck swept the land before him with a hard glance. "Who's orders?"

"Kelso's."

"Won't that put the stock pretty far from the ranch?"

Again the puncher nodded. "Just about as far as it can get, 'cepting the far-south line. Way we've been doing for years. Jim wants to give the grass along the high range a chance to grow back, get set for the winter."

"Makes sense on one hand," Shawn said, "but considering we're short of help, and everything that's going on, it don't on the other."

Tuttle flipped his cold cigarette into the night, settled himself on his saddle. "Come to think on it, it sure don't. Be mighty hard to keep tab on things—and if a man was to run into trouble, it's sure a far piece to the house."

"I'm changing it," Starbuck said. "Pass the word to the others. Morning comes, head the stock north for the hills."

Tuttle shrugged. "You're the boss. . . . What about Jim?"

"I'll tell him. Way I see it we're better off with everything—cattle, horses, and men, all bunched up as close to the ranch as we can get. We'll worry about grass later."

"Just what I'm thinking," Tuttle said, permitting himself to smile for the first time, and then touching the brim of his hat with a forefinger, he wheeled off into the darkness.

Shawn watched him fade into the night, and then sent the black on ahead, slanting now in the general direction of the river. A short time later he caught sight of the herd, or a fair portion of it, bedded down in a broad swale, in the lower center of which water stood in shallow depth. A campfire flared like an angry red eye in the blackness of the slope beyond the sleeping cattle, and he could see the vague shape of a man hunched nearby.

The remainder of the stock would likely be on to the south, he supposed, judging from what Rafe Tuttle had said. Either Jim Kelso was too stubborn for his own good in not moving the herd to a point where it could be more easily watched over, or else he was so worried and preoccupied with the problems besetting him that he was not thinking clearly.

That probably was it, and having no foreman to shoulder the responsibilities of the cattle, make the necessary decisions as to how the beef should be cared for, probably accounted for what appeared to be sheer carelessness—so obvious to an experienced man coming in from the outside.

He rode on, circling the swale, and came in to the fire. The squatting man drew himself erect and stepped back into the shadows of a doveweed clump.

"I'm Starbuck, the foreman," Shawn called.

At once the puncher reappeared, a squat, round-faced Mexican who cradled a rifle in his arms, and stared at Starbuck impassively.

"You Ortiz?"

"*Si, mi caporal*—Isidro Ortiz. I have wonder if you would come."

"Everything quiet tonight?"

"All is quiet. The cattle sleep."

"Going to start moving them in the morning," Shawn said, and repeated the instructions he had given Rafe Tuttle.

Ortiz made no comment. He simply nodded and waited in silence.

"How long've you worked for Three Cross, *amigo?*"

55

Starbuck asked then, staring out over the dark mass that was the herd.

"Three years, *senor.*"

"Then you know Jim Kelso and the ranch well. Can you tell me who is causing him trouble?"

Isidro shrugged. "This I do not know. Someone with a big hate for the *patron.*"

"A hate for sure—but why?"

Again the Mexican's shoulders stirred. "Who is to say? All are friends of the *patron,* yet there is one who is not a true friend, but a *lobo* who strikes when the back is turned. Who this is I do not know."

"You see any strangers around lately—a *vaquero* maybe?"

Isidro Ortiz once more moved his shoulders in the time honored way of his people, a gesture that meant little, meant much—and nothing.

"No, *senor,* no one."

Shawn smiled, said *"adios,"* and rode on. He was wasting time talking with Ortiz, doubted if he could supply any information of value, anyway. He was probably a good and loyal employee of Jim Kelso's but it would not go beyond that; he was one who would tend strictly to his own job, and close his eyes to all else.

Pete Helm was at the extreme southwest edge of the herd and came forward to meet him, gun raised. Tuttle had already given him word of Shawn's presence in the area, but he was one who took nothing for granted. When he recognized Starbuck, either by the horse he rode or from a description Rafe had given him, he holstered his weapon and sat back in silence.

Tuttle had advised him of the change in plan for the herd. If he approved or disapproved, he made no observation. He was content with giving monosyllabic answers to the few questions Starbuck put to him, and furnished no more helpful information than his two night shift companions.

Shawn turned then for the ranch and his quarters. He was discouraged in that he had failed to turn up one single thing of value that would enable him to get to the bottom of Kelso's troubles, but he felt the ride and time had not been entirely wasted.

He had looked over the herd, obtained a general view of the ranch, if at night, and met the remainder of the Three Cross crew; and he had made what he believed was a much needed change in the handling of the cattle.

What he wanted now was to sit down, mull it all about

in his mind, and see if anything emerged that would fit into some niche, perhaps make a little sense, and lead to a pattern. Once he could tie onto something meaningful, however small, he believed he could get on the right track. It simply made no sense that someone was striving to kill Jim Kelso, and destroy his ranch without cause.

But first he needed rest—sleep. He'd been a long time in the saddle. . . . Bed was going to feel plenty good.

═ 10 ═

Worn as he was, Shawn was up early, fully rested and feeling at his best. His pure, animal vitality had, in a few short hours of sleep, washed away the weariness that had finally overcome him.

He should first of all speak with Jim Kelso, he decided, and explain the change he had ordered and outline his reasons. The rancher had assured him he would not interfere with his way of doing things, but he still felt Kelso was entitled to know. Now, as he stepped out into the gray light of pre-dawn, he looked toward the main house. Lamplight glowed in the kitchen window and he could see Myra Kelso moving about.

Lambert, with Pierce and Dodd, appeared at that moment, coming from their quarters at a shambling gait, yawning, stretching, hawking in the way of men on their feet but not fully awake, and angled toward the cook shack.

Shawn joined them, greeting each with a short nod, and took his place at the oblong table where Candy had set platters of fried eggs, bacon, browned potatoes, and hot biscuits, backed with a pot of strong, black coffee. The meal was consumed in silence, and only when it was over did Starbuck give them his orders for the day on the moving of the herd.

"Tuttle and the others will stay out for a bit, help you get the stock turned and drifting. Be obliged if you'll carry some grub to them when you go. I'll be along as soon as I have a talk with Kelso."

Lambert wiped at his mouth with the back of a hand, pushed back his chair. "Reckon we'd best get at it. Ain't going to be no Sunday sociable—not with no more help'n we got."

The two other punchers got to their feet. Carl Dodd dug into his pocket for his pipe and said: "Not wanting to complain, but there a chance you can scare up some extra hands? These here long hours are about to lay me by the heels."

"Same here," Pierce said.

"Aim to try," Shawn answered. "Thing is I've got to

58

guarantee a man he'll live long enough to draw wages. Way it stacks up now I couldn't do that."

"I've got the feeling it's going to get worse," Lambert added morosely. "Them two trying to bushwhack Jim don't auger good. Been a lot of cussedness going on before but nothing like that."

"I got the same feeling," Pierce said. "Like maybe hell was about to cave in."

Starbuck watched the men stamp through the doorway, out into the yard, and veer toward the corral where Fermin had their horses waiting. In the attempt on Kelso's life they, too, were seeing the possibility of a showdown, and the resulting disclosure of whoever was behind it.

He would almost welcome it. As it stood now he was fighting a ghost, someone he could neither see nor antici- pate. If he could get Kelso's enemy out into the open, force him to tip his hand, matters would then be a lot easier since he would know who and what he was up against.

Nodding his appreciation for the good meal to Candy, who was busy at the moment assembling lunches for the crew, he rose, left the kitchen, and bent his steps for the main house. The side door was closed, and halting there, he knocked. It was opened immediately by Julie who greeted him with cool questioning in her eyes.

"Your pa—I'd like to see him."

Her brows arched. "Quitting—that it?"

Starbuck gave her a tight smile. "Not yet."

She unhooked the screen, pushed it open, and fell back a step to admit him into the large combination kitchen and dining room. Kelso and his wife were sitting at a table in the corner. A third chair, partly pushed away, indicated the girl had been seated with them. Myra Kelso smiled over her shoulder to him and the rancher beckoned.

"Come in—come in. Just in time for coffee."

Kelso seemed well recovered from his wound, and be- trayed no ill effects other than a carefullness in the way he moved his arm.

"Obliged, but I've got to get out on the range," Shawn said, and then told the rancher of the change he had ordered.

"Sounds smart to me," Kelso said when he had finished. "Figure you can handle all that stock with the men we've got?"

"Have to. Be hard work, but I think we can do it if nothing happens."

59

Julie, hands resting on the back of her chair, considered him quietly. "Just what could happen?"

Her hostility had not lessened, he noted. "Maybe nothing and most anything, ma'am."

The reply brought a tinge of bright color to her cheeks. "Don't you—"

"Now, Julie," Kelso broke in, "mind your tongue." He swung his attention back to Starbuck. "Could be I'll ride out a bit later, lend a hand."

"No, James," Myra Kelso said promptly and firmly, "you'll do no such thing. I'll not have you aggravating that wound."

"Well, there's nothing to keep me from helping," Julie declared.

Shawn stirred. Another rider would be most welcome, but he'd as soon it wouldn't be the girl. If trouble developed he did not want her on hand and in possible danger. He'd have more than enough to do without being forced to look after her.

"Not a very good idea," he said bluntly.

She folded her arms across her breasts, and gave him a steady, penetrating look. "Why not?"

"No reason I can say now, but—"

"Is it that you think I might see something that I shouldn't?"

"Now, Julie," Kelso began again in the same, placating way. "You know—"

"I mean it!" she broke in. "I don't think our new *caporal* wants me around because he's afraid I'll find out what he's up to!"

"Not that at all," Shawn said, hanging tight to his temper. "Just that if we do have trouble I won't have the time, or the men, to look out for you."

"I can take care of myself!" Julie shot back defiantly.

Jim Kelso pushed away from the table, chair scraping noisily against the floor, and got to his feet. "Starbuck's right. No place out there for you today. Something could bust loose, and I won't chance your getting yourself hurt."

"I'll be all right," Julie snapped, and spinning on a heel, marched from the room.

The rancher watched for a moment, then shrugged. "Bullheaded as she can be, that girl. . . . You go on, I'll try to keep her out of your way."

"For her good," Starbuck said. "That bushwhacker probably won't care which member of your family he draws a bead on next time."

"Know that, and like I say, I'll do my best to keep her

close, but if she shows up—well, look out for her. To hell with the cattle and everything else if it comes down to a choice. She's what counts with me."

Myra Kelso, suddenly worried, rose and went into the hallway down which the girl had disappeared. What Julie needed, Shawn thought grimly, was to be turned over somebody's knee and given what for; that would have been his parents' solution to what the rancher termed bullheadedness, and if she continued to act as she did toward him, by God, he just might undertake the chore himself!

To Kelso he said; "Don't want to have that come up, but that's the way it'll be, of course, if it does."

"Figured you'd understand. You think I ought to run into town again—if I use the buggy it'll probably satisfy my wife—see if I can hire on some hands?"

"Probably have no better luck than before. Nobody's going to sign on until they're plenty sure it's safe to work on Three Cross. . . . Doubt if it'd be smart anyway, your being out on the road."

Kelso shifted helplessly. "Dammit, feel like I'm caught in a box—"

"We get the herd moved to where it won't be so hard to look after, I aim to start digging into what's going on around here, see if I can put an end to it. Meantime, thing for you—your whole family—is to stick close to the house, not give anybody a chance to finish what those two started yesterday."

"Seems so—"

Shawn turned for the door, hesitated. "Whole crew'll be working for a while, so don't get to wondering why the night men haven't come in. By the way," he added as the thought came to him, "what about that outlaw? Anybody know him?"

"Nope," Kelso said, shaking his head. "Stranger to everybody. Deputy couldn't find a single solitary man who'd ever laid eyes on him before."

"Hard to believe. . . . Somebody had to hire him."

"What I thought—but that's the way things've been all along! Never able to tie down nothing!"

"Maybe it won't be that way much longer," Starbuck said, and went back into the yard. Crossing to his quarters, he dug into his saddlebags for the extra cartridges he carried. Taking a handful for his six-gun, he wrapped them in a handkerchief, thrust them into a pocket, and turned to go for his horse. He hauled up short.

A man—a *vaquero* by his gear, was standing in the

61

doorway. He was not old, probably in his thirties, was clean-shaven and wore cross-belted pistols. There was no way of knowing for sure but he looked to be the rider silhouetted on the *malpais* hill that evening before.

"*Senor caporal?*"

The Mexican's voice was soft edged, pleasant, yet there was a firmness to it.

"That's me."

"I am Pablo Mendoza. I have been told you are in need of riders. Such is true?"

Shawn considered the man narrowly. "The word's pretty well spread but there's no takers. You know the reason why?"

"There is trouble. This I was told."

"By who?"

Mendoza shrugged. "*Senor,* there are few who do not know."

Starbuck moved on into the yard. He could use a good hand, but he had doubts concerning the man. ... And if he were the one on the hill? ... He put the question to the *vaquero* bluntly.

"I see you up on the *malpais* last night?"

Mendoza's eyes flared slightly, and then a half smile cracked his lips. "Yes, I look at this place. A very beautiful *rancho,* owned by a fine gentleman, it is said. ... I think it would be good to work here."

"Kelso's needed hands for some time, and you've been seen hanging around. If you wanted work, why didn't you come ask about a job sooner?"

Mendoza shifted, and the sun, breaking over the hills to the east at last, caught the silver trim on his broad hat and made it glitter softly.

"A man must think well on such matters. It is not good to hurry."

"You ever work cattle in this valley?"

"In Mexico."

"How about friends—cattlemen—people who know you and will stand for you?"

"I have none here. I can give only my word, which is sacred."

Starbuck considered. He should probably leave the decision of hiring the *vaquero* up to Jim Kelso. But, when he gave it further thought, he realized that it was a part of his responsibilities, and what he was being paid for. He was supposed to use his own best judgment.

It could be a mistake. Mendoza was a stranger to everyone. He admitted being the one seen hanging about the place, had been in the valley for some time and never before sought work. Now he was asking to hire on at Three Cross. His explanation of the sudden change in attitude made little sense—at least to Shawn; but he had come up against the Mexican people enough to know their reasoning was not always logical to the mind of a Yankee.

And if Mendoza was a plant of Kelso's enemy, one sent there to become a part of the ranch someone hoped to destroy, would it not be better to have him close by, where he could be watched, rather than hiding in the shadows? The words of an old cowpuncher with whom he'd once worked came to Starbuck in that moment; *"long as I know where a rattlesnake is laying, I ain't ascared of it. It's the not knowing that rags my nerves."*

"You a good hand with cattle?"

Mendoza inclined his head slightly, once more setting up a shimmer of silver. His smile revealed even, white teeth.

"I am a *vaquero*," he murmured.

Shawn nodded. It was as good an answer and recommendation as he could get. "All right, you're hired. I'll get my horse and take you out to the herd."

"Muchas gracias," the Mexican said, turning toward his own mount. "I shall prove to you my worth."

=== 11 ===

Again on his own horse, the big, blaze-faced chestnut with white-stockinged legs, Shawn rode from the yard with Pablo Mendoza at his side.

"Moving the stock, or starting to," he said as their horses climbed out of the swale and broke onto the grass flatland lying to the south. "Want to push them up nearer to the ranch—along those hills in the west."

"The trouble the *hacendado* has—it grows worse?"

"Worse," Starbuck admitted. "Somebody tried to ambush him. He was shot in the arm."

A stillness came over Mendoza. After a few moments he said, "It is a sad thing that is happening to a fine gentleman. These assassins, did they escape?"

"One did. The other is dead."

"He is known?"

Starbuck shook his head. "Kelso had him taken into town. Nobody there ever saw him before."

Again the *vaquero* was silent. Finally, "It is the way of such men, strangers hired with money to do a job of killing—one who is sometimes known by my people as a *foraneo*—an outsider. . . . It is best that way for the one who wishes the death of another."

Shawn agreed. "You talk to somebody about Jim Kelso? Think you mentioned somebody telling you he was a fine man."

Mendoza said, "To the *muchacho* who works with the horses. He speaks highly of him, almost as if he was the father. Also it was he who told me where you might be found."

Starbuck looked away. He was getting no help from the *vaquero*. He had hoped the man had overheard someone speaking about Kelso, but that had not been the case. He glanced beyond the chestnut's head into the southeast. A dust cloud was lifting, beginning to hang over that section of the range. The crew had the cattle on the move.

An hour later he and Mendoza topped out a rock-studded hogback and looked down upon the herd. The brown haze stirred up by the churning hooves was so

64

dense that he could see only the puncher riding point, and the line of lead steers strung out across the front.

He had intended for the men to bear more directly toward the hills, get away from the bluffs that overlooked the river as quickly as possible—just in the event something went wrong. But he had not remembered to tell them, he guessed. It could be remedied quickly. He glanced to Mendoza.

"Ride down to the left, get between the cattle and the river. Want them turned more to the west. I'll carry word to the others."

The *vaquero* touched his hat brim, wheeled away, handling the close-coupled black horse he rode with ease and grace.

Starbuck struck off in a direct course for the rider at the head of the herd. As he drew near he saw it was Pete Helms. The weight of long hours on the job showed in the man's haggard features and in the heaviness of his eyes. He looked up at Shawn's approach, listened to his words, merely shrugging when told of the hiring of Mendoza. Then, swinging off, Helms spurred in alongside the old brindle steer that had taken over leadership of the cattle, and began hazing him in the direction of the low-lying peaks.

Shawn pulled away, curving around the mass of slowly moving animals. He found Lambert at swing position, and gave the word to him. Continuing on, he circled the entire herd until he met up again with Mendoza, trailing along at drag just outside the boiling dust.

"It goes well," the *vaquero* said, pulling his bandana down from his mouth and nose. "There is never trouble with the cattle when they have full bellies. They are like sheep."

"Hope they stay that way," Starbuck commented.

It would require most of the day to make the transfer, he had figured, after looking over the range that previous night, and at the herd's present pace it would appear that he had estimated correctly. Later on in the day they could expect the steers to move faster, even if the grade increased. They would be hot and thirsty and the smell of the upper sinks and water holes in their nostrils would act as a goad.

Suddenly there was a shifting in the herd. It was as if some powerful force had collided with the opposite left flank, causing the right to bulge. Shawn whipped away, cut toward the rear of the heaving mass. Gunshots sounded then, lifting above the dull thudding of hooves. In the next moment he saw a bright flash of fire through the yellow haze.

Fire—but how?

He didn't wait to ponder the question, just roweled the gelding hard, sending him plunging into the wall of spinning, swirling dust that blanketed the cattle. A rider loomed up, saw him, swerved in close. It was Carl Dodd.

"Stampede!" the old puncher shouted. "Whole tail end of the herd!"

Starbuck cursed. "Stampede!" he echoed. "How the hell could—"

"Somebody filled a wagon full of hay—set it afire and turned it loose at the cattle!"

That was the flash of flame he'd seen through the pall. "How bad?"

"Don't know for sure," Dodd answered, fighting his panic-stricken horse. "Got the wagon stopped—had to shoot the horses. . . . There's maybe four, five hundred steers legging it straight for the bluffs."

"Who's over there?"

"Ortiz and Pierce—and me. What I come for—help. Need it bad."

Shawn made no answer to that, simply rode in beside the older man, and with him wheeled toward the river and the rim of the buttes rising above its west bank. It would be up to the four of them to stem the onrushing tide of frantic steers; the others would be needed to keep the remainder of the herd under control.

Shortly, Starbuck caught sight of the running cattle. They weren't moving fast but at a more set, determined pace. Ahead of them he could see the two riders whipping back and forth, firing their pistols. The steers seemed neither to hear nor see them.

Shawn reached back for his blanket roll, swore as he remembered removing it along with his saddlebags at the ranch. He threw a glance to Dodd, began stripping off his shirt.

"They're crazy blind! Got to catch their eye somehow—flag them down!" he yelled. "Use anything you're packing. Only way we can turn them!"

Waving his shirt madly, Starbuck cut directly in front of the pounding cattle. Pierce, face caked with sweat and dust, gave Shawn an understanding look and twisted about. Digging into his leather pouches, he produced a dirt-streaked white towel. Swinging it over his head, he spurred toward the leaders of the stampede.

Dodd was also moving in for that point, an old shirt

wigwagging in his hand. Uncertainty began to show in the front-running steers. Several attempted to veer, were caught up by those pressing in close behind, carried on. But the break was there. Seeing it, Shawn wheeled the chestnut about to right angles, driving straight into the teeth of the cattle.

Again the leaders faltered, swerved, were crowded on by the mass behind. Several managed to turn, and the forward momentum of the mass slowed. Suddenly an entire segment began to curve away. Dodd was upon them at once, waving his flag, and firing his pistol.

Shawn hauled the blowing chestnut about, stiffening as alarm rocked through him. The lower part of the splinter herd—a hundred steers or so—were still racing in a direct line for the bluffs. Pierce and Ortiz were slicing back and forth, doing their utmost to turn the bunch into the others, force them to follow the main body. But it was a losing battle; the lip of the bluffs was too near.

"Get out of there!" he yelled, standing up in his stirrups. He knew he'd not be heard above the hundreds of pounding hooves, but the warning came out anyway.

Pierce and Isidro Ortiz recognized the danger. In another few moments they would be trapped, caught between the edge of the cliffs and the oncoming herd. Both spun, jammed spurs to their horses, and bent low over the saddle, rushing to get out of the cattle's path.

They made it with only a stride to spare—and then the bawling, struggling mass of hooves and horns was pouring over the bluff to the ground fifty feet below.

Grim, Starbuck rode slowly to where the two men sat in stunned silence staring at the empty flat. The sounds of the dying cattle seemed distant, almost muted. Pierce turned to him as he came up, and shook his head.

"Done all we could—reckon it weren't enough."

"No fault of yours," Shawn said, brushing at the sweat and dust clouding his eyes. "We got the biggest part of them turned in time."

"Was maybe a hundred head there—all prime beef. You be telling Jim about it?"

"I will," Starbuck said in a clipped voice. "You two go on, help with the others. I'm going to do some looking around."

"For what? There ain't nothing—"

"That wagon had to come across here somewhere. Couldn't have driven it in from the north—we'd have seen it. And they never brought it through the hills. Too

67

damned rough. Leaves only the river—and there ought to be tracks."

Dodd pursed his lips, nodded. "About right. Expect I'd best tag along, however. Isidro can give the boys a hand."

"No!" Starbuck's reply was unduly sharp, but the loss of the steers and the possibility that at last he might be in a position to uncover the identity of whoever it was dealing all the trouble to Kelso, was pushing at him hard. "Better if I go alone. If things get tight I can move about easier."

"Just what they'll do! We ain't dealing with no green-horns—made up my mind to that when Jim got hisself shot up. Man doing what you aim to do sure ought to be sided."

"Maybe, but I'll make out. Be more of a favor if you see to it the herd gets to that valley close to the hills."

Dodd shrugged, spat. "Whatever you want."

"That's it," Shawn said, and pulled away.

The bawling at the foot of the bluff had all but ceased, and he guessed most of the animals were dead. He swore deeply, angrily, thinking of the waste. . . . A hundred good steers—food now for the buzzards and the coyotes.

Riding on he came to what he sought, a break in the bluff. At once he saw the neat, flat grooves of a wagon's iron-tired wheels, together with a welter of hoof prints. All led up from the river.

Descending the wash, he reached the flat lying between the ragged-faced formation and the stream easily follow-ing the wheel's imprints to where the vehicle had emerged from the silted water. Dismounting, he squatted, studied the marks of the horses carefully, striving to determine the number of riders there had been in the party. It was impossible to tell. Prints were everywhere—and there were none with distinguishing characteristics that would aid in locating the owner.

But one thing was certain—wagon, riders and all, had come from Las Cruces. The wheel grooves made that a foregone conclusion. Accordingly, it was simple logic to assume the men who had been involved had by then or were at that moment returning to the same point. . . . But he should be sure of the latter.

The hoof prints where the wagon entered the river all pointed in the direction the vehicle had taken. The riders had apparently forded the broad stream at a different place on their return. Mounting, he continued along the soft bank, eyes searching the moist soil. Within a short distance he pulled the gelding to a halt.

The tracks of three horses, walking abreast, came out

of the shallow water, crossed the narrow beach, and disappeared into the brush. Starbuck swung onto them, following them with no difficulty to where they reached, and turned into the road. A hard grin pulled at his lips. The riders were heading for Las Cruces, as he had anticipated. Roweling the chestnut, he set out in pursuit at a fast gallop.

12

He slowed the gelding to a walk at the south end of the settlement, and came to a full stop when he turned into the main street. There were no horses moving along the curving roadway that separated the double row of business houses, and he had not overtaken any riders on the way in. Evidently they were much farther ahead of him than he had thought.

Regardless, they were somewhere in the town, and there was nothing to do but search about until he found them. It shouldn't be too difficult; simply locate three horses that showed signs of having recently forded the Rio Grande—caked mud on their legs, still wet cinches, stirrup leather dark from water.

Easing forward on the saddle, he hitched his pistol to where it rode a bit higher and was more accessible, then clucked the chestnut into motion. Keeping to the right-hand side of the street, he moved on, eyes cutting back and forth, probing the animals pulled up to the various racks.

There were several saddled mounts, along with two or three wagons and buckboards, in the yard behind Hunick's store. He veered into that enclosure, made his careful inspection of the horses, and returned to the street. None of them appeared to have been in the river.

His roving glance came to a stop on the mounts in front of the Spanish Dagger. One had a definite caking of mud along its fetlocks. Shawn looked closer. The belly of the bay alongside it had a coating of tan, as if the hair had been wet and then sprinkled with dust. He could get no good look at the remaining animals.

Swinging past the saloon and the adjoining Amador Hotel, he rode in behind the structures. Tension was beginning to build within him, and he found himself touching the nearby area with a sharp glance, searching for men who might be the riders of the horses.

He still wasn't completely sure; he'd have a closer look at the animals standing at the rack, and if he discovered one more showing signs of having been in the river, he felt he could then be fairly certain he had found the men responsible for the stampede, and, logically, for the attempt on Jim Kelso's life and all the other woes that had befallen Three Cross.

The hostler appeared in the doorway of the Amador's stable, an expectant expression on his swarthy features. Shawn waved him off, guiding the gelding into the rack provided by the hotel for riders just dropping by for a brief visit with its tenants.

Dismounting, he made fast the chestnut's reins. Nerves taut, he moved to the corner of the building where he could get a better look at the horses in the street. There was a third one, standing slack-hipped among the others, that definitely had been in the river.

Starbuck needed no more. Anger now lengthening into a cool, steady pulse within him, he drew back, prepared to circle around and enter the saloon by its rear door. He hesitated, an ingrained respect for the law, and all it stood for, surfacing within his mind.

He should bring Dave Englund into the matter. After all, the deputy ought to handle it—an opportunity he likely would welcome, since the law had maintained it needed only something of a definite nature to bring it into the situation. But the need to locate Englund quickly was urgent; the three riders could slip away, and with them would go the one opportunity he had for clearing up Kelso's troubles.

Brushing at the sweat collected on his face, he pivoted, walked back in behind the Amador once more, and moved by the chestnut into an inset of other structures littered with discarded packing boxes, whiskey kegs, and wind-blown trash, pointing for an adjoining passageway that led to the street.

He slowed as the rear entrance to one of the smaller saloons standing farther down swung open, and two men swaggered into the enclosed area—two men both vaguely familiar at first glance, and then as they drew nearer, fully recognizable. Dallman and the Kid. Shawn swore softly. He had given the pair no more thought after getting what he believed was a glimpse of them in the street that day before; it would seem, however, they had devoted considerable attention to him.

The older man brushed his hat to the back of his head, hooked his thumbs in his gun belt and grinned broadly.

"Seen you prancing around here. . . . Proved what I told the Kid yesterday—that we'd be meeting up again. . . . Told you that, didn't I, Kid?"

The blond, taking no chances, had already drawn his

71

pistol and leveled it at Starbuck. He nodded, an eager glint in his eyes.

Shawn glanced around. He had no time to waste on this pair. It was imperative that he find Englund, take him to the Spanish Dagger, and make his accusations against the men he'd trailed into town before it was too late.

"Move on," he said impatiently. "I'm in a hurry. Forget this until the next time we meet."

Dallman laughed, winking broadly at the Kid. "You hear that? He's in a powerful big hurry right now. Was in a rush yesterday, too, when he stuck his nose in my business, and got poor old Charlie and Waldo killed."

The Amador's hostler appeared again, coming out onto the hardpan fronting the double door. He glanced curiously toward them. Shawn raised a hand to signal but the man turned away in the same instant, and ambled off in the direction of the hotel.

Grim, angered at the interference, Starbuck brought his attention back to the outlaws. "You want trouble with me—all right. But not now—later. Got a chore to do that can't wait."

"The hell it can't!" Dallman snarled, dropping his bantering manner. "Hold that iron on him, Kid, while I draw his fangs. Then we'll take us a little ride into the hills. Ain't nobody pulling what you did on me, mister, and getting away with it!"

There was no avoiding the encounter. He could only hope the three riders in the Spanish Dagger did not leave. Settling himself squarely, Shawn watched the outlaw move toward him. A few steps beyond, the Kid waited nervously, the tall hammer of the pistol in his hand pulled to full cock.

Dallman, a crooked grin on his face, halted in front of Starbuck. "I'll just take that there hogleg you're wearing," he said, and reaching for the weapon hanging at Shawn's hip, plucked it from its holster.

Starbuck's hand was like a striking rattlesnake. It flashed out, caught Dallman's wrist, and clamped down with the force of an iron-jawed vise. In that same instant he threw his weight to one side, spinning the outlaw about.

"Goddammit—shoot!" the outlaw yelled, dropping the pistol.

The Kid rushed forward. Shawn, still holding to the older man's arm, released his grip, heaved Dallman straight into the oncoming blond. The pair coming together with solid impact, rebounded.

72

"Shoot!" Dallman shouted again, floundering on hands and knees.

The Kid recovered his balance, and triggered his weapon. The explosion set up a deafening echo in the pocket between the buildings, and the bullet made a hollow, slapping sound as it buried itself in the wall behind Starbuck.

Instantly he lunged forward, caught Dallman just as the man was regaining his feet, and sent him stumbling once more into the younger outlaw. As both went down, he wheeled, scooped up his own weapon, and then closed in on the pair scrambling to disentangle themselves.

Snatching Dallman's pistol from its leather, he threw it into the piles of trash. Wrenching the one held by the Kid from his fingers, he tossed it into a close-by rain barrel. And then, breathing hard, he looked down at the two outlaws.

"I'll say it again—I've got no time now for you. Later—if you think you've got a call coming—"

"Now!" Dallman yelled furiously. "We're settling it right now!"

Before Shawn could move, the man flung out his arms, caught him around the legs. Heaving to one side, he dragged Starbuck down. Striking out at the distorted face pressed close to him, Shawn tried to break the grip locked tight to him, tried to pull away. In the next moment he felt the Kid slam into him, and then all three were prone in the dust.

Lashing out with a knotted fist, Starbuck broke clear. He rolled to one side, jerked away as Dallman kicked out with a booted foot, winced as he felt a blow to the head. Twisting, he saw that the Kid, with that same wild, eager light in his eyes, had bounded upright, and was boring in, both fists flailing.

Throwing himself backward, he spun to his feet, came erect, and meeting the Kid with a stiff left arm, stalled him abruptly. In the next instant he became aware that Dallman was also up and surging in. Spinning, Starbuck unconsciously dropped into the cocked stance of a trained boxer—arms in front of him, elbows crooked, knotted fists poised.

He surprised Dallman with a hard left, crossed with a right to the ear that dropped the outlaw to his knees. The Kid, recovered, was rushing in from the side. Starbuck, neatly sidestepped the blond's awkward approach, caught him by the collar and belt, and taking a few accompany-

73

ing steps to increase momentum, sent him reeling headfirst into the nearest wall.

Rock-hard knuckles smashed into Shawn as he whirled. He felt his knees buckle and his senses drift, but only briefly, and as he sank he allowed himself to fall away from Dallman, now standing over him and hammering blindly with both fists.

Suddenly he ducked forward, came up under the outlaw's arms, crowding him close. Dallman, hindered, sought to back off, to free his movements. Starbuck seized the slack in his shirtfront, rocked back and pivoted. As the outlaw, badly off balance, fought to retain his footing, Shawn drove a savage right into his jaw.

Dallman seemed to pause, a dark, wondering frown on his sweat-streaked features as he hung there. Starbuck, pressed by his urgency, lashing out with a vicious left, nailed the man with a hard right. Dallman wilted, took two or three backward steps and collapsed into the trash piles.

Shawn turned quickly, once more retrieved his dropped weapon, aware for the first time of the dozen or more men gathered about. Ignoring the hurried rash of congratulations and aside comments, he started for the Spanish Dagger. There was no time left now to find Dave Englund; he would have to act on his own.

"Hold on there, Starbuck—or whatever you call yourself!"

At the command Shawn stopped, turning slowly. It was the deputy. Englund had his pistol out and was moving up cautiously. Apparently he had been standing in the crowd watching the encounter.

"Was aiming to get you," Starbuck said, eyeing the lawman narrowly as he endeavored to assess his intentions. "Trailed three horses in from Kelso's. Men riding them are some of the bunch who've been—"

"Sure," Englund cut in drily. "Suppose you just raise your hands. No tricks now; I'd as soon shoot a killer as jug him."

Shawn stared. "Killer—me?"

"Nobody else but," the deputy said, glancing around at the crowd of surprised, silent men. He was enjoying his moment of eminence, there was no doubt of that. Stepping up to Starbuck he lifted the tall rider's pistol from its holster and thrust it under his own belt.

Anger brushed aside the astonishment in Shawn. "You're way out in the woods, Deputy. If you're aching to do some arresting, take in these two," he said, ducking his

74

head at Dallman and the Kid. "They tried holding up the west-bound stage yesterday. The driver and guard'll tell you that when they come in again."

Englund nodded genially. "That so? Well, I'm obliged for the information. . . . Seems I'm going to have me a whole jail full of desperate outlaws waiting for the sheriff when he gets back. . . . Two road-agents and a killer, my—my!"

Starbuck swore angrily. "Climb down off that high horse, Deputy!" he snapped. "There's three men inside that saloon that've got to be arrested. They stampeded Kelso's herd this morning. Caused a hundred or so to go over the bluffs. You've been yapping about needing something to go on before you could give Kelso some help— I'm offering it to you now."

"Could be," Englund said with aggravating disinterest. "Point is, I've got you three—and like they say, a bird in the hand is worthy a plenty in the bushes." He looked around at the crowd again, making the most of his moment. "What I'm doing now is take you over to the lock-up, and put you in a cell where you can cool your heels until the sheriff gets back."

"You fool around acting biggety," Starbuck cut in, "and those three I told you about will get away. First chance we've had to nail whoever is giving Kelso trouble, and you sure as hell had better not muff it!"

"I get your under a lock, then maybe I'll look into it," the deputy said grudgingly.

"You're a fool—a damned fool!" Starbuck raged, anger boiling over. "Forget that pair of two-bit owlhoots, and the two of us can go in there, grab those—"

"One thing at a time—that's my motto," Englund prattled. He made a gesture with his pistol at Dallman and the Kid. "Come on you jaspers, I'm marching you and this here killer over to my jail."

The accusing word slashed through the yellow haze that was fogging Starbuck's mind. It was the second time the lawman had called him that.

"Killer—who am I supposed to have killed?"

"Who? You trying to say you don't know?"

"Be a favor if you were to tell me," Starbuck replied sarcastically.

Dave Englund cocked his head slyly. "Maybe it'd be better was I to call you by your real name."

"Starbuck's the only one I've got."

"The hell it is! Your right name happens to be Friend—

75

Damon Friend, and you're wanted for killing a man right here in town."

Shawn stared at the deputy. A rumble of conversation swept through the crowd.

"Either you're loco or—"

"Just telling you the facts," Englund said with a wave of his hand. "Sheriff's been looking for you ever since. Bud Kitch, the jailer, recognized you yesterday when you come in. Then I watched you fight these two—all that fancy dan way of using your fists and dancing around. One of them professional boxers, ain't you?"

"I've been taught—"

"Ties right in with what Kitch told me. Said you looked like the killer—and the killer was one of them boxers. All adds up—and there ain't no doubt in my mind. You're Damon Friend."

The crowd had grown considerably, and comments were becoming louder, assuming a threatening note. Several men now suddenly remembered Damon Friend and the exhibition he had staged, the fact that he had later killed someone. ... Dave Englund was sure a good man, right on his toes. ... Bud Kitch, too. ... Morrison ought to be mighty proud of his deputies. ...

Shawn, jaw clamped tight, studied the lawman while the irony of the moment spread through him. He was being mistaken for the very person he had come to inquire about—a skilled boxer he hoped might be Ben.

In that next instant, realization flooded through him. This man they were talking about—this Damon Friend— *was* Ben! That name, Damon, from the old legends of the Syracusans—Pythias and his friend Damon—it had been one of his brother's favorite stories when they were small boys at their mother's knee, listening to her read from the books she so treasured.

That remembered fact, plus the apparent resemblance, and the statement that the man sought was a trained fighter, could be added up to but one conclusion; he was at last definitely on Ben's trail!

76

═ 13 ═

Kitch, sweating freely, shouldered his way through the crowd. Brandishing a sawed-off shotgun, he stepped in beside Englund, bobbed his head approvingly.

"Got him, eh? Mighty fine. . . . Who's these others?"

"Tried holding up the Tucson stage, according to Friend. Aim to lock them up until George Eberhardt gets back to town, see if there's anything to it."

"And him?"

"Locking him up, too, of course. Claims he ain't the bird we're looking for—but they all say that. We'll keep him in the cooler for Morrison. I'll take a run down to El Paso this afternoon, soon's it cools a bit, and send him a telegram, tell him what we got."

The jailer nodded again, made a sweeping motion with the old double-barrel. "All right, you jaspers, start walking—"

Starbuck turned toward the passageway that led to the street, fell in behind the Kid and Dallman, who was cursing steadily in a low monotone. He glanced in the direction of the Spanish Dagger, to the men gathered there. He recognized the bartender, Gentry, and the gunman, Vern Ruch. The others he did not know and could only wonder which among them were the three he had trailed from Three Cross range.

Sudden frustration rushed through him. He whirled on Englund. "Dammit—those men will be getting away unless you move in—"

Kitch pulled up short, weapon leveled, stiffly alert. The deputy laid his hand on the barrel, pushed it down, and shook his head at the jailer.

"They'll keep," he said then to Shawn. "Keep moving. I got you, and that's what's counting with me. Like I said, a bird in—"

"Oh, go to hell," he muttered in total disgust, and continued on. A moment later he added: "That thick skull of yours is going to get you in a bale of trouble. Those three I keep harping about are the ones doing all the

77

damage at Kelso's. Likely one of them is the other bush-whacker that tried to kill him!"

Englund's features betrayed some reaction to that. He frowned, looked over his shoulder at the horses tied to the saloon's hitchrack.

"Which horses you meaning?"

"The gray, the buckskin, and the sorrel with the hair bridle. Can see they forded the river."

The deputy shrugged indifferently. "They's a lot of riders ford the river around here, instead of using the bridge."

"Whoever's riding those three horses are the men I trailed from Kelso's, after they started a stampede."

"You see them—the men forking them?"

"No, were too far ahead of me. I'm going by the fact that the horses had just waded the river—were still wet when I caught up."

"Ain't much to go on," the deputy mumbled. "Maybe I'll see about it."

"You're a fool if you don't," Shawn replied and lapsed into silence. He could see little use in wrangling further with Englund.

They reached the jail. The deputy stepped out ahead, entered, and drew back the doors of two of the three cells. Kitch herded Dallman and his young partner into the first, Shawn into the second. Englund slammed the gratings closed, turned the locks. Tossing the keys onto the desk, he placed his attention on the jailer.

"I'm walking over to the Dagger, see if there's anything to what he's yapping about. Now, mind you—don't go getting yourself tricked while I'm gone."

Kitch's features darkened. He wagged his head. "Ain't nobody ever fooling me again."

"Just be damn sure of it. Stay plumb away from them, hear?"

"I hear," the older man mumbled, and watched the deputy pass through the doorway into the open.

Starbuck, anger undiminished, felt better. At least he'd accomplished that much—persuading Dave Englund to check on the riders. Next thing to do now was consider his own predicament. He must convince the deputy he was not the man the sheriff wanted, and get out of the cell. He was needed at Three Cross—needed bad, he was certain. The stampede had convinced him more than ever that matters for Jim Kelso were drawing to a head.

Mopping at the sweat gathered on his face, he stepped close to the bars, and waited for Englund's return. It

78

would be most difficult to prove his innocence he realized; the entire matter of his being cleared would rest with Sheriff Morrison, and he was absent—days away.

Even if it were possible to find a local resident who had seen Damon Friend, and would declare Englund and Kitch wrong, the deputy would undoubtedly refuse to accept the person's word, and not release him until the sheriff himself approved.

There was only one solution—jailbreak. Englund was planning to make the ride to El Paso and send word to Morrison of the arrest he'd made. That would require the afternoon, possibly most of the evening. Kitch would be in sole charge. He'd watch the old man, see if he could spot a weakness, a carelessness that would lead to an idea.

"Ain't forgetting this, cowboy—"

At Dallman's low voice, Shawn turned to face the man. The heat in the small building was murderous, and he brushed again at the sweat beads on his forehead and the moisture filming his eyes.

"Got you to thank for being in this goddam, two-bit jailhouse. Sticking your nose in my business yesterday, then shooting off your mouth out there today. . . . I'm owing you plenty."

"Any time you're ready to pay off, I'll oblige," Starbuck said coolly. "Doubt if you'll be getting much chance, however—not where you'll be going."

"Hell, way it looks you'll be right alongside me and the Kid—"

"Don't bet on it. Deputy's made himself a big mistake."

Dallman grinned, winked at his partner. "Tried that myself a couple of times. Never did work."

"Will for me," Starbuck said. "Happens to be the truth."

"Well, won't make no difference. No matter whichaway it goes, I'll be laying for you, Starbuck or Friend or whatever your name is—and you can figure on it."

Shawn was barely listening to the threat. He was watching Bud Kitch, remembering the words of caution Englund had spoken to him. The jailer was slouched in the chair behind the desk, his tired, moody eyes on the dusty street. It was near mid-day and the sun was relentless. Indifferently, he brushed at a fly buzzing about his sweat-glistening face.

"You figuring how to bust out of here?"

It was Dallman again. Starbuck only stirred.

A coyness came into the outlaw's tone. "You do, count

me and the Kid in, and I'll forget what I was saying about evening up with you—"

Boot heels rapped against the landing outside the door. As Shawn once more sleeved away sweat he watched Dave Englund enter, hauling up in the center of the sweltering room.

"What about it?" he demanded impatiently.

"Like I thought—was nothing to it."

"What the hell's that mean?" Starbuck shouted angrily. "I trailed those three—"

"Wasn't them," the deputy interrupted calmly. "If it ain't a crock of bullchips to start with, it was somebody else you tracked. These fellows rode in from up Socorro way. Names of Jennings, Palmer, and Duncan. . . . Know any of them?"

"Never heard of them. What'd they say about fording the river?"

"Didn't deny it. Seems they crossed north of town."

"You believe that?"

"Sure. Was some others seen them doing it."

Shawn settled back dissatisfied. It was hard to believe he had made a mistake—even in the face of witnesses.

"Who saw them? It somebody whose word's good?"

"About as good a witness as a man could ask for; Omar Gentry. He seen them. Didn't know them, he said, but he recollected the horses."

Starbuck turned away wearily. He'd been wrong, he guessed. Three men had ridden off Kelso's range after starting the stampede. They'd crossed the river and started for town—but there everything certain ended. Evidently the outlaws had swung off the road somewhere between the point where they had reentered it and the settlement. He had missed that, had continued on, and spotting the mud and water-spattered horses in front of the Spanish Dagger, had jumped to a conclusion.

"Reckon I slipped up somewhere, Deputy," he said. "Followed three men, just like I said. Seems I lost them somewheres on the south road. Might pay you to do some looking down there."

"Be no use. Lot of brush—even an Indian couldn't find nothing in."

Shawn gave it up. "You heard anything from the Kelso place?"

Englund ran his finger along the inside of his collar, easing the sweat band. "Not since Felipe hauled in that dead man last night."

"Was plenty of trouble out there this morning. You

80

want proof of it, ride down to the bluffs, take a look at the steers piled up at the bottom. Looks like that ought to be enough to bring the law in—or is somebody going to have to kill Jim Kelso first?"

"One of them things," Englund said, refusing to rise to the mockery in Starbuck's voice. "Can't stand around out there and wait for something to happen. Got others folks to look after. . . . I'm ready to step in alone, or with a posse, anytime Kelso's got somebody for me to go after. . . . All we ever hear is a long tale about something after it's done with."

"Sounds like the law around here wants folks to do its job for them, then holler. Put a special deputy on the place, let him hang around."

"Takes money for that—and anyway, that's something Kelso ought to do—hire himself a gun . . . Dammit, Kitch," Englund broke off irritably, mopping at his face, "why don't you prop open that there window? Like an oven in here."

Wheeling, he stamped toward the door, then halted. "I'm going to get a bite to eat. Soon's I'm done I'm lighting out for El Paso. Won't be no hotter riding than standing around here. . . . Think you can look after things while I'm gone?"

"Sure—"

Dallman suddenly rattled the door to his cell. "How about some vittles for us, Deputy? Or maybe this one-horse burg don't feed the prisoners."

Englund favored the outlaw with a contemptuous look, then resumed with the jailer. "I'll have Segura send some grub over for you—and them. That all right?"

"Reckon so. . . . Old woman was expecting me home, but I guess it don't make no difference."

"On my way out I'll drop by and tell her. I ought to be back about dark."

"Take your time," the jailer replied, disinterestedly.

"Just what I aim to do—hot as it is. . . . Now, you watch yourself!"

"Sure, sure," Kitch muttered, and as Dave Englund stepped out into the streaming sunlight, added, "Goddammit, a man stubs his toe once and nobody don't ever let him forget it. . . . Hell of a note."

The afternoon hours passed with frustrating slowness. The heat, trapped inside the jail, was suffocating, and when sundown finally came and the sun's driving lances no

81

longer battered the walls and roof of the squat building, relief was immediately noticeable.

Starbuck, a caged, impatient animal, failing to devise any means for escape, stirred restlessly about in his cell. He felt utterly defeated, yet beneath it all a curious elation flowed; he was finally on Ben's trail. Previously there had been only rumors to go on—vague hints, tips, hearsay, but this was solid—definite. . . . And he had a name.

All he need do was wait until Sheriff Morrison returned, which he likely would now do within the week, let the lawman see that his deputies had made a mistake and locked up the wrong man—and then free, his cash-money reserve built up somewhat, resume the search.

Only he couldn't just sit back and let it work that way. He couldn't afford to wait. He had responsibilities to Jim Kelso, a fine, if somewhat ineffectual gentleman, who was in over his depth, fighting a losing battle against a ruthless, unknown enemy. He had made his commitments to the rancher and he would not welch on them.

Somehow he must break out, return to Three Cross as fast as possible. This could be the very night the final blow would be struck; with Kelso more shorthanded than ever, as well as personally wounded, it offered someone an ideal opportunity.

Dropping onto the hard slat cot, Shawn stared moodily at the door of his cell. The rectangle of bars fit snugly in its frame and there was little chance it could be pried open at the lock—even if he had something with which to pry. His eyes settled on the lock. Hope stirred within him.

Rising, he moved to the front of the cell. In the next cubicle the Kid and Dallman, their faces shining with sweat, snored deeply. In the chair at the desk Bud Kitch also dozed. Shawn glanced toward the street; he must do something soon; Englund would be returning and his presence would make an escape much more difficult.

Bending down, he reached into his left boot, procured the slim-bladed knife carried there in a leather sheath. Opening it, he probed the lock with its point. Satisfaction rolled through him. There was a chance—a good chance, but he'd have to get Kitch out of the way. Concealing the knife, he leaned up against the grillwork.

"Jailer!" he shouted.

Kitch jumped a little, roused, and sat up. "What do you want?" he demanded peevishly.

"Time we ate—"

The jailer glanced to the street, now darkening as night

began to settle over the town. "Got to wait for the deputy."

"Wait—hell!" Starbuck yelled, making a noisy issue of it. "It's supper time. Was only about half enough on that plate at noon to keep a man going. I'm plenty hungry and I'm not about to wait. No reason why you can't get something for us now."

"There sure ain't," Dallman, awake, chimed in. "That deputy ain't apt to get back much before midnight."

Kitch struggled to his feet stiffly, mopped at his face. "Well, you got to eat, that's for certain. Don't see as it makes no difference whether it's now or later."

"It's being hungry now that counts."

The old jailer walked out from behind the desk, and crossing to the door, halted. Looking back over his shoulder, he said, "Don't go raising no ruckus while I'm gone, now—or you won't get nothing. Hear? You do and I'll throw it to the dogs."

Dallman laughed. "Why, grandpa, we'll be quieter'n a mouse. You'll see!"

Kitch spat, then stepped out into the street. Lamps were glowing in windows and a mellowness had spread over Las Cruces, bringing a peaceful sort of suspension, a time at which, it seemed, all things were pausing to rest.

"You wanting him gone so's you can bust out, that it?" Dallman asked as soon as Kitch was beyond hearing.

Starbuck made no reply. Opening the knife, he bent down once more, examined the lock more closely. It was one of the old drop-slide type, activated in the usual manner by key insertion. . . . If he could find enough slack in the framework to wedge his knife point under the tongue, he should be able to flip it back.

Glancing at the doorway to be certain no unexpected visitors or passersby were in evidence, or that the jailer was returning ahead of time, Shawn began to work the knife blade in under the oblong of iron. The lock was heavy, crudely cast, with more thought given to weight than to a fine job of finishing. He found considerable looseness, and managed to find purchase for the blade's point in the rough surface of the metal.

"Getting it?" Dallman asked anxiously.

Shawn paused, looked again to the doorway. All was clear. Careful, he pressed gently, levering the knife. The tongue flipped back into its slot with a dull thunk.

"You done it!" Dallman said in surprised tone.

Ignoring the man, Starbuck slipped the knife into its sheath, once more looked to the street. Kitch would be

83

showing up shortly. There was no time to lose. Opening the cell door quickly, he ducked low to avoid being seen through the window, and hurried to the lawman's desk. Pulling out the top drawer where he had seen Englund drop his pistol, he recovered it and slipped it into his holster.

"The keys—the keys—" Dallman called hoarsely. "Goddammit, throw me the keys!"

"Make it fast," the Kid added, speaking for the first time. "The old man'll be coming."

Shawn, still paying no attention to the pair, crossed to the door, peered cautiously around the frame. Except for three men standing in front of Amberson's Gun Shop, the street was deserted.

"Ain't you turning us loose?" Dallman's tone carried a plaintive note.

Starbuck faced him. "No—you're outlaws, I'm not. You belong in there."

Dallman's features contorted with rage. A string of oaths burst from his lips. "Goddam you—you lousy bastard—I'll remember this! I'll—" Abruptly the harsh words broke off. A change crept into his tone. "Hell, no reason for you to do this to us. We can be friends. ... Tell you what, throw me them keys and I'll forget what I said about squaring up with you. That a deal?"

"You're talking to the wrong man. It's the law you've got to do your bargaining with," Shawn said and turned again to the door.

Once more checking the street and finding it empty, Starbuck stepped into the open, and with Dallman's curses following, swiftly circled the jail and gained the alley behind it, where he could not be noticed by Kitch or anyone else who happened to make an appearance.

The outlaw's voice was lost to him here, and walking fast, he went along the littered corridor to a point below the Spanish Dagger. He paused there, threw his attention to the hitchrack. The three horses were gone, he saw—not that it made any difference. Crossing over in the shadow of a large cottonwood, he reached the yard behind the Amador. The chestnut was waiting patiently at the rack where he had been tied, and mounting, Starbuck cut back and rode out of town—a hope burning within him that Dave Englund would not return for a few hours more, at least, and thus stay from underfoot.

He could not shake the hunch that the situation at Kelso's was building to a violent climax, and try as he would, he could think of no decisive way to meet it,—fight it off—and that for the solitary and simple reason that he could find no enemy to engage. It was a frustrating experience, like shadowboxing, where a man lashed out, but found only emptiness.

He came to the point along the bluffs where the steers had thundered over the edge. As he paused and looked down, lean shapes were moving among the carcasses, and faint snarls and growls came to him. The coyotes hadn't had it so good in many a day.

Pulling away, he struck off on a long tangent for the upper end of Three Cross range, where the herd should now be bedded down. He rode steadily but with a certain caution, eyes and ears alert, ready to halt, challenge, draw his weapon at the slightest provocation.

Nothing interrupted the crossing, however, and he came finally to the long, grass-covered ridge lying south of the valley into which the cattle had been driven. Drawing to a halt beside a scrub cedar, he looked down into the swale. Two fires were visible, one on the east slope, one below, and to his left—the south. He grunted his approval. Lambert and the crew were playing it as carefully as they could, setting up their watches on the two sides where trouble, if it came, would first present itself.

Cutting right, he followed along the ridge for a short distance, and then slanted down into a short saddle that connected with the ridge lying along the basin's east side. Gaining that border, he pressed on, the flickering flames of the fire only a short distance away. Relief was flowing through him now; evidently all was well with the herd.

He pulled up short, a faint sound catching his attention. Instinctively his hand swept down to the pistol on his hip—and then fell away as he heard Pablo Mendoza's voice.

"Senor caporal."

Silent, he watched the *vaquero* materialize from the darkness of a cluster of dense catclaw. "Hell of a good way to stop a bullet, *amigo*," he said, weariness and impatience edging his words.

Mendoza's teeth showed white in the murk. "There is no good way for that, my friend—only bad. You have luck in finding the *malhechors* who slaughter the cattle?"

Starbuck shook his head. "A long story. Men I figured were the ones I tracked from here, turned out to be somebody else—according to the deputy. Fellow they call Gentry saw them crossing the river north of town."

"Gentry." Mendoza mouthed the name thoughtfully. "He was the one to give proof?"

Shawn studied the *vaquero*. "He's the one. You know him?"

The Mexican shifted, laid his hand on the oversize horn of the intricately decorated saddle he sat. "I have heard of him. . . . These others—was mention made of their names?"

Starbuck continued to watch the *vaquero* closely. It seemed to him the man's questions carried something more than idle curiosity; they had, in fact, a meaning of importance to him.

"The deputy called one Jennings. And there was a Palmer. Third man's name was—uh—let's see—"

Shawn labored to recall, purposely creating an opening for Mendoza. The man failed to rise to the bait; either he did not know the outlaws, or was too wise to be taken in by the trick.

"Duncan," Starbuck finished. "That's it, Jennings, Palmer, and Duncan. Were supposed to have come down the valley from Socorro. Know them?"

"I do not, *senor*," the Mexican said quietly.

86

A moment later Shawn dropped his gaze and looked off across the valley. There was no prying anything out of Mendoza unless he wished to give it, that was certain.

"Have any more trouble with the cattle after I left?"

"There was none, and all is good now. We have been in this valley since dark."

"Rest of the crew on the job?"

"The old and the one that limps, they sleep. At midnight they will come that the others may also sleep."

"And you?"

"It is something I have small need for. I have learned to sleep while I am awake—if such is possible to understand. So I was when you came. I sleep but there is enough of me awake to know of your coming."

Starbuck nodded. He had acquired much the same facility himself. "Works for me, too," he said, lifting the chestnut's reins to move on.

"The young *muchacha* asked for you," Mendoza said. "Also the *patron* himself. They were disturbed that you are gone so long a time."

"Was in jail, most of it," Starbuck said.

The *vaquero* leaned forward, peered at him. "In the jail?"

Shawn smiled. "Another long story," he said. "See you in the morning," and rode on.

The ranch was in complete darkness when he entered the yard and halted at the entrance to the barn. Dismounting, he led the gelding through the open doorway, headed him into the first empty stall, and removed his gear. There were grain and fresh hay in the manger, and the big chestnut had previously watered, thus obviating that chore. Retracing his steps to the hardpack, Starbuck made his way to his quarters. . . . So far his hunch had been wrong; both the herd and the ranch itself were untouched and peaceful. He could only hope there would be no change.

He realized how utterly beat he was when he stepped into his cabin. It had been a long, hard day replete with tension, violence, worry, and sapping heat—all of which were dragging at him now, filling him with an exhaustion that overrode even a need for food.

Striking a match to the lamp on the table, he sat down on the edge of the bed, fought with his boots until they came off, and then lay back, stretching himself crossways upon the crackling mattress. He felt his gun digging into his side, realized he had forgotten to remove it. Sitting up slowly, he flicked back the buckle's tongue, stripped off the belt, and hung it on the bedpost.

87

He sat for a time thinking the smart thing to do was pull off his clothes, crawl into bed properly, instead of waiting, resting—but once more he gave way to the easier course. . . . He'd get to bed right in a minute—just as soon as he—

The door creaked. Unmoving, and instantly alert, he cracked his eyelids. A sigh escaped him. It was Julie Kelso. Patient, he drew himself to a sitting position. The girl, her face angry, was holding a rifle in her hands, had it leveled at his chest. The round O of the muzzle looked as large as a silver dollar.

"Put that damned thing down," he said wearily.

Her eyes flamed brighter, the curves of her lips compressed into a straight line. He considered her for a moment, stirred resignedly.

"What is it now?"

"You've got a lot of gall coming back here!" The words burst from her, lashing him like small pellets.

He moved gently, not at all at ease under the threat of her rifle. She had the hammer pulled back—and the trigger spring could be a worn and touchy one.

"Where'd you expect me to go? I work here."

"Not any longer—not if I have anything to say about it!"

"Which you haven't," Starbuck said bluntly. "It's your pa that I—"

"I know—he hired you and it'll have to be him who fires you—and that's just what he'll probably do. We know what happened. Aaron told us all about the fire and the stampede and the cattle that went over the cliff. . . . Then you disappeared. Going to hunt down the men who did it, you claimed. I want to know one thing—you find them?"

Julie's words were coming out in a rush, trumbling over each other in her haste to say them. She was under a terrible strain and deeply worried, Shawn realized, and a wave of sympathy swept through him.

"Sure didn't. Thought I had them but—"

"What I expected!" the girl cried triumphantly. "It was all just a reason to get off the place, report to whoever it is you're working for, get more instructions."

"Instructions?"

"Don't play stupid! Instructions on what you're supposed to do next. The stampede only partly worked. We lost only a hundred steers. . . . What's it to be now?"

Shawn got to his feet slowly, daring the rifle. Anger born of exhaustion, and the girl's unreasonableness,

88

whipped through him, and he was too tired to care much about anything—particularly what she had to say.

"Now?" he snapped. "I'll tell you straight, I figure to nail up all the doors in the house, set it afire, and then—"

"You would, too!" Julie broke in, tears flooding into her eyes. "It's what I'd expect—"

Starbuck's hand streaked out, clamped about the rifle's action, blocking the hammer and preventing its accidental discharge. Julie relinquished her grasp on the weapon, stepped back, battling a fresh onslaught of tears.

Silent, Shawn released the rifle's hammer, propped it against the bed as he considered the girl. She was bearing far more of the load than she deserved. With an indecisive father, a mother who could not or would not recognize the problems and dangers that faced them, a crew of old men who could be depended upon for little more than tending cattle, and trouble striking from all points, there was small wonder she had no faith in him.

"Know it's been hard on you," he said. "Want you to know I'm doing all I can to straighten things out. You've got to believe that."

Julie didn't look up. "I wish I could—"

"You can. I hired out to your pa to do a job. That's the same as a promise, far as I'm concerned—one I'll keep no matter what comes along."

She shook her head. "Everything's going against us—everybody—even you. Actually it has grown worse since you came."

"Could be another reason that's got nothing to do with me. May be that whoever is back of it all is getting to crack down hard, make his final move."

Julie gave that sober thought. "It's possible, but why? What does he, whoever he is, want?"

"That's the question I keep asking myself. What it is Kelso's got that a man is willing to go the limit to get? There's an answer somewhere but I can't find it."

She had dried her eyes and recovered some of the hostility that had fled under the surge of tears.

"You have a strange way of hunting it—and trying to help. You even hired that *vaquero*. I don't trust him—nobody does."

"You know anything against him?"

She shook her head impatiently, dismissing in a woman-like way the necessity for such facts. "He's a *vaquero*, and that's enough. He's been hanging around doing nothing all this time, and then when he asks you for a job you put

89

him right on. Why would he suddenly want to go to work?"

"Could be he ran out of money. Happens to me every so often. That the only reason you don't trust him?"

"The fire and stampede happened right after he rode out on the range with you. It could be—"

"Mendoza was with me when it started. He couldn't have had anything to do with it."

"He could have arranged it beforehand—had those men start the fire—"

Starbuck shook his head in irritation. "He could have but I'm betting he didn't. There's something that's not exactly clear about him, I'll grant you that, but I don't think he's had a hand in the trouble you're having. And if I did, I would've hired him anyway. Easier to keep an eye on a man working for you than one hiding off in the brush."

"Still think you're wrong," she said truculently.

"All right, go ahead," he replied tiredly, and turned from her. "Now mind getting out of here and letting me get some sleep? Been up since four this morning and I—"

He heard the door slam and looked around, surprised. It was a strange, new experience, having Julie Kelso comply without an argument.

═ 15 ═

Jim Kelso stood at the kitchen window and stared out across the low hills toward the river. In the raw light of early morning the grass had a glazed, silvery look, and the trees assumed a ghostly quality. It was yet an hour or so until daylight, but he hadn't been able to sleep. The wound in his arm had throbbed insistently; however, the discomfort arising from it was much less than that provoked by his own conscience.

How could his world change so swiftly, so completely? Only a few months ago all had been serene. He was a successful rancher, the Three Cross brand was widely known, and held in high esteem by everyone in that part of the land; men, neighbors, his wife and daughter, the hired help—all looked upon him as a person of character and achievement.

But none of them had known the real Jim Kelso—a man who discovered one day that he lacked the courage to face adversity for the simple reason that he did not know how.

Life in the beginning had been pleasant and easy. His share of the family estate in Kentucky had provided money to marry on, move west, and buy up sufficient acreage to start a ranch. Land was cheap, and there'd been enough money to also procure a fair-sized herd of cattle as a nucleus, erect comfortable, weathertight buildings, and start off better than the average would-be cattle grower.

Raising beef had proved a success from the start. The market was good, the first two winters extremely mild, and he'd cashed in handsomely. Everything had gone just right, and it seemed he could do nothing wrong. He had the touch, Myra had declared proudly several times, and so it seemed.

But then came the day of change. He couldn't quite remember exactly when it was—about three months ago he thought. First there was that fire, one of the line shacks on the west range. He really hadn't worried about it. Accidents did happen; a cowhand, or possibly a drifter, careless with a match or a cigarette, or perhaps it had been a party of Mexican *bandidos* crossing the border and venting their spite on a *gringo hacendado*. He'd brushed off the incident.

And then a few days later a water hole had been poisoned, several steers died. He had to face up to it then, admit it was no accident; the act was deliberate. He had known a flash of panic when he realized that, but he'd been careful to mask it from Myra and Julie, who always seemed to think that all he need do was snap his fingers and everything would be set aright.

He'd made a show of talking to the hired help, telling them to keep their eyes peeled, and he'd taken to wearing the pistol he'd bought years ago but hardly knew how to fire. The atmosphere around Three Cross sort of improved and he entertained the thought—a hope, really—that all trouble, as some ancient philosopher once noted, would pass.

It was not to be. A week later a half dozen cattle were driven into an arroyo near the bluffs, and slaughtered. Several of the ranch hands, hearing the shots, had ridden over to investigate. Before they reached the spot guns opened up on them. No one was hit, but the net result was that every man involved quit. They'd not hired out to have lead thrown at them, they declared.

Desperate, a large herd on his hands and only half enough riders to handle it, he'd gone then to sheriff Morrison, and laid the problem before him. It was the natural thing to do, place it in the hands of the law. ... Only Morrison didn't see it in exactly the same light; he couldn't figure out any way he could help, unless Kelso could pin down the source of the trouble—tell him who to go after, and why.

He just couldn't keep a deputy quartered at Three Cross, hanging around drawing wages while he waited for something to happen. The county just didn't furnish that kind of money. ... Find out who was at the bottom of it and he'd damned quick go after them.

Thus the law had proved of no assistance and the depredation and vandalism had continued. More of the help quit until now only the old hands remained—out of loyalty, he liked to think, but he knew it was likely because they had nowhere else to go.

Fortunately he managed to get a large part of the herd sold off, and that eased up on things considerably, and while that portion remaining was still more than the few old cowhands he had working could manage efficiently, they were, with his help, and that of Julie, getting by. One thing good about it, Julie had come to take a great deal more interest in the actual operation of the ranch than she had previous to the start of the trouble.

In a way that pleased him. It was a needed change, yet he secretly regretted it. It would have been a fine thing if she'd been able to retain her illusions as to his infallibility. But he supposed, like all pleasantries, everything must one day end. He only hoped that seeing him in his true light, ineffectual, unable to cope with the reversal of fortune that was plaguing him, she would not turn entirely away.

There was a good chance he could yet pull it all out of the fire. This man Starbuck, the new *caporal*, struck him as one not likely to be pushed around, and if anyone was going to be able to get to the bottom of Three Cross's trouble, he'd probably be the one—assuming he managed to stay alive long enough.

Whoever was gunning for him and the ranch wasn't letting it go at small fires and killing off a few steers anymore. The ambush and the stampede proved that, and he was glad that Starbuck had overruled his suggestion to drive into town, and had instead, insisted that he not again expose himself. . . . Somebody was out to kill him. . . . That was a hard fact now. . . . But who—and why?

Abruptly distraught, Kelso turned away from the window, crossed to the big cooking range that dominated the southeast corner of the room. Earlier he had stuffed a few short lengths of split piñon wood into the firebox, set them to blazing, and now the pot of coffee he'd made was simmering busily. Taking up the gray enameled pot, he poured himself a cup.

He could hear Myra moving about in the bedroom. Julie would be up soon, too. He didn't feel like facing either of them. Walking softly in the wool felt slippers Julie had presented him with last Christmas, he left the kitchen and entered the small room adjoining that he had converted into an office. Closing the door, he slid the bolt and sat down on the edge of the desk. Nursing his coffee, he once again turned his eyes to the yard.

The crew, if it could be called such, had already wolfed their morning meal, were riding out to relieve the men who had been with the cattle during the night. He watched as Candido appeared, apron swept aside and tucked into a hip pocket, dish pan of water in his gnarled hands, and dumped it against the cottonwood growing alongside the cook shack. . . . Candy was getting old, walked with legs crooked, back bowed. He'd not noticed it before.

He was getting up in years, too, he realized—and that

was something he hadn't really become aware of. It was a strange thing, but a man wasn't conscious of that fact until he saw it in his friends.

A gentle tapping sounded at the door, and then Myra's voice asked him what he'd like for breakfast. He passed it off, saying he was not hungry, that he would get something later. He was thankful she accepted that and retired without attempting any persuasion.

His thoughts shifted once more to Shawn Starbuck. He wondered what had happened to him. Lambert said he'd gone after the outlaws who had caused the stampede, was hoping to track them down. Shawn hadn't returned at sundown, and Julie, who for some reason did not trust him, had prophesied they'd never see him again, that he, like all the others, was gone for good. She firmly believed him to be part and parcel to all the trouble they were experiencing.

Julie could be right, he had to admit it—but he was hoping that she was not. Starbuck was the sort of man he liked having around—the kind he wished he himself might be: hard, strong, quick, and not afraid of the devil with both hands full of brimstone. . . . He'd walk over to Starbuck's quarters to see if he'd come in during the night. The prospect wasn't too promising; if he had caught up with the men he was trailing, word would have reached the ranch before then.

Kelso sighed wearily. He'd had high hopes after seeing Starbuck in action there in Coyote Canyon, but now it would appear, as Julie had insisted, all that had been for show, pure window dressing as a means of putting himself in solid at Three Cross. . . . It was hard to believe. He'd always considered himself a pretty good judge of men, but—

The rancher's thoughts came to a stop as his eyes caught sight of a buggy wheeling into the yard. He recognized the light rig immediately—one of the rentals that could be hired at Celso Mondragon's livery stable. The man driving—round, fleshy-face, trim dark suit under a tan duster, rolled brim hat—was familiar. The vehicle drew nearer, halted at the short rack outside the office door. The driver wound the reins about the whipstock, climbed down slowly, stiffly. Kelso remembered in that moment; Blaisdell, the El Paso banker.

Frowning, he stepped to the door, opened it. Blaisdell, smiling in a cordial, businesslike fashion, entered, extended his hand.

"Glad I caught you," he said. "Got in last night. Drove

out early this morning on purpose. Wanted to catch you before you rode out, have a little talk."

"Was about to leave," Kelso replied for something better to say. Blaisdell's visit was a surprise. He thought he'd seen the last of him. "What brought you all the way up here?"

"You," the banker said, settling into a chair, "and that client of mine. He plain won't give up. Still wants this place. Insisted I pay you a call, repeat his offer."

"I see," Kelso murmured, leaning against a corner of his desk. Here could be the out he'd secretly, in the bottom of his mind, hoped for—an easy solution—sell. Leave the country, let someone else take on the grief. Myra likely would oppose it—and Julie most certainly would, but they could be won over. All he need do was point out they were not the ones who had to face the bushwhackers.

"Well, could be I'm interested."

"Thought perhaps you might be. Heard at the hotel last night you were having a spot of trouble."

"Other ranchers have seen worse—and it'll pass. Hired myself a new *caporal* a couple of days ago. Plenty sure he'll straighten things out."

"Good. Then I can tell my client you'll consider his offer?"

"Consider, yes. No promise now, mind you, but I'll study on it. Have him put it in writing, send it to me by coach mail—no need you making a trip."

Blaisdell got to his feet. "He'll be pleased to hear you've changed your mind."

"Not definitely," the rancher said, deeming it wise to play it coy. "I'm saying I'll consider it—not exactly take it—not yet, anyway."

"I understand, and I'll make it clear. It's more than I came away with last time. Making some progress, it seems."

Kelso nodded. "Well, man gets older, starts to thinking about a rocking chair, taking it easy—"

"In only three months?"

"In three months," the cattleman said solemnly. "Things can change fast. Folks do, too. ... You never mentioned that client's name before. Care to now?"

"One thing that hasn't changed—he still wants it kept quiet. Business reasons, he tells me. Seems he's interested in other properties and is afraid his name coming into the open might pose a problem or two."

"Could be," Kelso said, then, as a thought stirred

through the back of his mind, added, "He want my place pretty bad?"

Blaisdell cocked his head to one side, and smiled. "You expect me to answer that?"

Kelso caught himself just in time. He had wondered if the party concerned could desire the property bad enough to apply pressure in such a way as to influence the selling, but he realized in the same instant that he could not possibly voice such a thought.

"Reckon not," he replied with a forced laugh. "Would be worth my knowing though, wouldn't it?"

"To you—but it could cost my client a pretty penny. Sorry I can't give you his name."

"Don't matter. One man's money is as good as another's far as I'm concerned."

"Which is a sound rule of business," Blaisdell said, moving toward the door. "He'll be pleased to know you've changed your thinking about selling—"

"Not for sure," the cattleman cut in quickly. He'd have a job convincing Myra and Julie that it was the thing to do, and while outside events were dictating that he move as quickly as possible, he wouldn't be able to rush matters too much where his womenfolk were concerned. "Want you and him, whoever he is, to understand that. I'll consider his offer—and I'm leaning toward selling. That's as strong as I'll go right now."

"Exactly what I'll tell him," the banker said, climbing into the buggy. "Well, hope to see you again shortly," he said, unwinding the lines he settled back against the cushions. "Good day."

Jim Kelso lifted his hand, but his thoughts were already speeding ahead of the moment. He'd market the herd, turn the beef into cash money. That, with what he had in the bank was more than he and his family would ever need. Then he would accept whatever price for the ranch itself that Blaisdell's client wanted to offer—and be pleased to get it. . . . But first there was the matter of selling Myra and Julie on the idea—and even that required courage.

Julie Kelso had risen early, too. Disturbed by Shawn Starbuck, in a way she had never before known, she sat at the window of her room and looked into the yard, unseeing, unhearing, existing only in her thoughts.

In her mind she knew all the things she had accused him of were groundless, yet her strong pride would not let her admit it even to herself. The life of Three Cross

96

literally rested on his shoulders, in his strong hands, and finally having accepted that truth, she wished now she might break down the barrier that lay between them—and tell him so.

It was folly to think her father would be able to bring an end to the creeping death that was slowly overcoming the ranch. He seemed helpless to fight, to do anything other than stand by and permit it to happen. Shawn was the only man capable of stepping in, setting everything straight, and she was in no way helping, but actually hindering him by accusations, by being disagreeable and opposing him—and by telling him to his face that he was unwanted.

What ailed her, anyway? What perversity of mind caused her to berate and disparage and insult the only man who had ever aroused her inner self—and who likely was the sole hope of the Kelso family and Three Cross?

She saw the door to Starbuck's cabin open, sat up straighter, watched him step out into the yard and swing across the hard pack in that confident, easy way of his. He'd not taken time to shave, and there was a rough, square look to his jaw, while his deep-set eyes—sort of slate gray, she recalled, now appeared dark.

Something within her seemed to convulse, and the inclination to hurry out—robe, nightgown, and slippers be damned—tell him she was sorry, that she regretted all she had said to him, possessed her. And then Rafe Tuttle and Carl Dodd, followed closely by Dan Pierce, came from the bunkhouse and joined him. The impulse faltered.

Later ... she'd make her apology later. She'd wait and watch for him, catch him when he rode in at the end of the day. Or maybe she'd just saddle up and run out to where the herd was being grazed. It wouldn't be hard to talk to him there.

═ 16 ═

No problems developed during the night insofar as the herd was concerned, Lambert told him, and a short time after Ortiz, Mendoza, and the old puncher, who had stood watch the final hours of the shift, had ridden in, Shawn mounted the chestnut and pointed for the valley where the stock was being held.

He couldn't expect to keep the cattle there for any extended length of time, he realized as the gelding loped leisurely across the grassy plains and saddles. The basin simply wasn't large enough and the steers would soon have it grazed over.

Perhaps the emergency would have passed before that time came. ... Emergency. ... He considered that word. What emergency? Certainly there were the baffling incidents that took place periodically, the most serious of those being the attempt on Jim Kelso's life, but actually, when you came right down to hobnails, he was taking precautions against a hunch.

He didn't really know something was about to occur. He had only a feeling, an intuition, one based on perceding events. It could be that matters would rock along now for another month or two before something would break. ... If he could believe that, depend on it, there'd be no use in keeping the cattle penned in the basin. Might as well let them drift as usual, scatter over the range.

But Shawn couldn't bring himself around to where he accepted that. A deep worry, small but persistent, continued to nag at his mind, filling him with a sort of apprehension, almost a fear, for what lay ahead for the Kelsos. He could not ignore it, no matter how hard he tried.

Long ago he'd learned the value of trusting his instinctive insight and the wisdom of heeding its warnings. With matters the way they stood at Three Cross, and that feeling nagging at him now, he suddenly decided he'd be a fool to ignore any premonition, however groundless it might seem.

He drew near the valley, and the bawling of the cattle came to him. But it was a sound of contentment rather than of restlessness and he was not concerned. Reaching the east rim, he rode slowly along the rounded ridge, waving his salutations to the men cruising aimlessly but with effective purpose around the herd.

Kelso had a fine ranch, there was no denying that fact. Plenty of acreage, year-round water, ample grass—all in a country known for its mild winters and not too extreme summers. It was a place some man might conceivably want badly, but there were many other ranches in the valley like it, equal to, possibly even better in some respects.

Why, then, had Kelso's ranch been singled out as a target for so much trouble and disorder? What was it about Three Cross that made it more desirable than all others—so desirable that murder was not to be bypassed? There had to be a reason.

He'd gone over the question countless times before, and now fell to pondering it again as he ranged back and forth across the hills and shallow valleys looking for something, for anything that would throw light on the puzzle and furnish him with an idea.

He had halted at the edge of a small grove around mid-afternoon, and was still threshing the problem about in his mind with no success, when Julie Kelso topped a knoll to the east of him, and came riding up.

Shawn observed her approach with a jaundiced eye, recalling their previous encounters and the bitterness of her words. He'd hoped that she would leave him alone, permit him to do his job as best he could, but he guessed it was not to be.

She was especially attractive today, he noted, watching her draw nearer, sitting the saddle of the gray she rode with a calm, easy assurance. And as before, when he looked steadily at her, the manliness of him stirred and some of the loneliness he had known in the long nights of the past, made itself felt.

But just as on similar occasions before, he thrust such human and personal needs aside; he could never expect to choose a wife, a partner for himself, settle down and have a home, a family as did other men, until he found Ben and squared the matter of their father's estate.

That moment could come that very day—or ten years in the future—there was no way of knowing. Someday, somewhere, he would meet with Ben, or find him dead, and then the quest would be over. But until that time he must deny himself the life other men took for granted.

"Good morning—"

Julie's voice was friendly, had a cheerful quality. Starbuck felt a trickle of relief; evidently she was not here to castigate him. Removing his hat, he stepped from the saddle and walked to the gray's flank, and helped her dismount.

She smiled her thanks to him and crossing to an outcrop of nearby rock, leaned up against it. "I came to apologize," she blurted hurriedly, seemingly anxious to get the words out and have done with it before courage disintegrated.

He studied her, understanding. "Not necessary," he replied in an offhand way. "We both want the same thing. Knew that from the start. Was just that we saw it different."

"I know," she murmured. "But I'm sorry about all the things I've said to you. . . . I've been afraid to trust anybody."

"Natural. Can't blame yourself for that. Three Cross is a fine ranch, and the way things are going—" He let his words trail off, seeing no point in reminding her of the danger her father, and probably she and her mother, were in.

She did not miss his meaning. "We could all be ambushed—killed. I know that."

Starbuck was silent and then shook his head in a show of helpless exasperation. "Trying to prevent anything like that. Spent the whole day so far covering the range, trying to see what's behind it all. Came up with nothing—but there has to be a reason somewhere, and I'm too blind to see it!"

"I know," she said wearily. "I've lain awake nights thinking, hoping to understand. . . . It's all so senseless—and hopeless."

"Not yet. We're still on our feet and we've managed to survive eveything that's been thrown at us so far. If I could just come up with one thought—"

Julie, hands clasped before her, stared out across the flat unrolling before them, a far, distant look in her eyes. A faint breeze had sprung into life, and the tips of the grass were shifting gently to and fro, turning the land into a purple-tinted ocean.

"It may not matter now, anyway."

Starbuck frowned in surprise. "What's that mean?"

"Maybe somebody else will have to worry about Three Cross."

"Your folks thinking of giving up?"

"Not exactly—selling out. Blaisdell, that El Paso banker, came to see my father again this morning. Man he represents is still interested in buying."

Shawn brushed at the sweat on his brow thoughtfully. "You said again—he the one who made your pa an offer a while back?"

"The same. Was about three months ago."

"Thought the name sounded familiar. He mention this time who he was making the offer for?"

"No. My father asked but Mr. Blaisdell said he had to keep it quiet. Something about some other property he's interested in, and this could maybe spoil it for him."

"And your pa's going to accept his offer?"

"He hasn't said so yet. He told Blaisdell he'd think about it. Last time he turned the idea down."

"You think he'll accept?"

"I—I guess so, the way things are going. We have plenty of money and my folks are getting along in years. Why should they put up with all this trouble, this risk of getting hurt—or worse?"

"Can see their point. How do you feel about it?"

"Not my place to have any feelings on this."

"Maybe not, but I'd like to know, anyway."

"I'd not sell—I'd fight. I love Three Cross and I can't imagine what it will be like not to live on it. I don't think any other place could ever be home—but it is my father's decision. He'll do what he believes is best and I'll abide by it."

She drew away from the rock. Starbuck dropped back, allowed her to pass before him and cross to where the gray waited.

"No matter how it works out," she said, halting beside the horse, "I want you to know that I think of you as, well—more than just somebody who came to work for us. I—I only realized that this morning." She paused, color rising in her cheeks. "I hope I'll continue to see you, that we—"

Starbuck stepped into the breach of her confusion, took her by the arm and assisted her onto the saddle. As she settled herself the small rowels of her spurs jingled lightly.

"I hope so, too," he said gravely, and then as if the thought was only then occurring to him, "Blaisdell's first offer, how long ago did you say it was?"

She stared at him with stricken eyes, cheeks mirroring the embarrassment that flooded through her. She had bared her heart to him and he had discreetly ignored it.

"Three months, more or less," she said tonelessly.

His features were void, deliberately betrayed nothing.

"Do you remember if the trouble started after that, or did it begin before the offer was made?"

She had regained her composure, and now her dark, full brows arched into a frown. After a moment she said: "I see what you're driving at—that maybe it's Blaisdell's client who is stirring up trouble for my father, trying to force him to sell."

"That's what I was wondering."

"It started before Blaisdell came to see father, I remember. . . . I'm sorry."

He only shrugged. "So am I. Could have been the answer we're looking for, or a step toward it, anyway."

Julie studied him for a long moment, her eyes wide, lips firmly pressed together, and then she said: "Does it really matter now?" and cutting the gray about, started down the slope.

Starbuck watched her ride off, pointing for the ranch while a heaviness filled him. He did not like the role he'd been forced to play, but it was best. He could not permit anything stronger than a casual friendship to rise between Julie and himself. . . . Only after he found Ben would his life be his own.

He started to move back to the chestnut, paused, realizing that the time factor in the offer made to Jim Kelso could mean nothing. Blaisdell's client could have created trouble beforehand in hopes of getting a quick and favorable decision from the rancher. And, that failing, he had simply continued his ruinous activities.

He remained motionless watching Julie fade into the distant trees, and then, wheeling to the gelding, stepped up into the saddle. The chestnut was anxious to be off and struck out at once with no urging, his long, white-clad legs flashing rhythmically as they covered the ride in a proud stride.

An hour or so later Shawn hauled him in once more. His gaze had caught sight of a rider far down the slope, working in and out of the trees and brush. It would not be one of the cowhands working Three Cross beef; the swale where Kelso's cattle grazed lay far to the north and west.

A drifter? Not likely—not in this particular part of the range. This was someone who knew the area, had ready access. He appeared to be searching for something.

Thoughtful, Starbuck watched the rider break from the last of the brush fringing a grove. Sunlight caught at the man, pinned him sharply with its brightness, stirred a sparkle of silver. Shawn stiffened. Mendoza was the only rider on Three Cross wearing such ornamentation. He continued to study the *vaquero*, amending his previous impression; the Mexican seemed to be patrolling rather than searching.

He kept Mendoza in view for a time, and then cutting down into a shallow ravine that slid off to his right, began to follow. He could not see the *vaquero* too well as he rode in and out of the undergrowth and occasional patches of trees, and as the minutes passed, the wonder grew within him as to the man's purpose.

Certainly it was possible for a person to mount his horse and ride across the range for the sheer pleasure of doing so—but Mendoza had been with the night crew and it didn't seem reasonable he'd be spending the day in the saddle, also. Ordinarily most cowhands were glad to pile off their horses, and stay off during their leisure hours, having had all they wanted of a saddle while on the job.

His earlier suspicion of Mendoza surged to the fore. There was something about him that wouldn't stand the light—he was sure of it now. That conviction settled in Starbuck's mind, and being a man who disliked subterfuge in all its forms, plagued with the seemingly unsolvable problems that beset Jim Kelso, he came to a sudden, angry decision. There was some connection between Pablo Mendoza and what was happening to Three Cross, and the way to get at the bottom of it was to confront the *vaquero* bald-faced.

Starbuck's jaw clicked shut, and roweling the chestnut, he set the big gelding to a fast lope, aimed at intersecting the path the Mexican was following a mile or so below.

Mendoza heard him coming, drew in behind a clump of doveweed. Shawn caught the hard glitter of silver through the leaves, as he broke over the last ridge and drove down into the small valley.

Halting at the edge of the growth he said, "You figure to hide from a man, best you trim those silver gewgaws off your *sombrero*."

The *vaquero* walked his horse into the open, his dark face expressionless. "I do not hide, *senor*, only wait."

Starbuck shrugged. "Call it whatever. . . . Thought you'd be grabbing some sleep."

The Mexican shifted on his saddle, stiffened his legs. The *tapaderos*, thickly scrolled and decorated with leather rosettes, were large as water buckets.

"I am one who needs but little sleep."

"So you told me—now tell me something else."

Mendoza's expression did not change. "What is that, *caporal?*"

103

"What's going on here at Three Cross? You've got something to do with it. I want the whole story—now!"

The *vaquero's* hands lifted and fell in a gesture of bewilderment. "I know nothing—"

"You have anything to do with that ambush? You in on killing Three Cross beef—burning line shacks—all that hell-raising that's going on?"

Mendoza's face was a sullen image carved in dark mahogany. "I am not a man of that kind," he said stiffly.

"But you know who it is!" Starbuck snarled. "Spit it out, *compadre,* or I—"

"The *muchacha,* she comes. She brings with her the deputy from Las Cruces—"

At Mendoza's interruption, Shawn twisted about. Julie, Dave Englund at her side, was approaching at a fast lope. It could mean only one thing; the deputy was there to arrest him, take him back to a cell. He swore deeply. He had no time for that now—had hoped to avoid the law until matters were cleared up for Kelso. After that he'd be willing to go in and square himself.

"All a mistake," he said to the *vaquero.* "Wants to lock me up, but I'm not about to let him. Important I stay on the job—"

Starbuck paused, the feeling coming over him that he was alone. He turned to the doveweed where Mendoza had been. The *vaquero* was no longer there.

═ 17 ═

Starbuck lifted his gaze, picked up the figure of the Mexican disappearing into a deep ravine. He swore again. That was proof enough, he guessed, that Mendoza was involved.

Angered, he swung his attention back to Julie and the lawman, now drawing close. If they hadn't showed up when they did he might have gotten something out of the *vaquero!* Stiff, he watched them pull up. There was a shine of moisture on the girl's forehead and a strained, worried look in her eyes.

Englund, hand resting on the butt of his pistol, met Shawn's gaze coolly. "You coming peaceful, or do I have to take you in?" he demanded with no preliminaries.

Starbuck glanced to the sky. The afternoon was late and sundown not too far off. With darkness, the trouble he had been expecting could strike. Mendoza's actions now heightened that belief.

"Forget it, Deputy," he said quietly. "Do a little thinking about the Kelsos. If it pans out like I think, they'll need the both of us here."

Dave Englund's mouth drew into a hard grin. "One thing they sure don't need is a killer hanging around, making things worse."

"Wrong man, Deputy," Shawn said patiently. "I'm not who you think I am."

A sort of relief came into Julie Kelso's eyes. Her lips parted into a smile. "I knew it! I knew you were wrong, Dave! Shawn's no murderer."

Englund shrugged. "You expect him to admit it?"

Julie nodded. "Yes, I think he would, if it was true."

The deputy favored her with a direct look. "You'd make a mighty poor judge, but I reckon that goes for any woman. A bit of sweet-talk and they'll swallow anything."

"Wasn't that," she replied. "Just that I know."

"No matter," Englund snapped, swinging his attention again to Shawn. "I'm locking you up, Friend—"

"Name's Starbuck—"

"May be what you're calling yourself now, but the real

105

handle's Damon Friend. Sheriff'll verify that when he gets here next week. . . . Let's go."

Starbuck, glancing at the girl, wished she wasn't there. Making a fight of it would endanger her and this he could not bring himself to do. Locked in a cell, however, he'd be powerless to help the Kelsos if a raid was launched that night.

"I'm sorry, Shawn," Julie murmured, as if reading his mind. "He insisted that I take him to you. My father thought it best, too. . . . He told us you were a murderer, that you broke jail."

"Was in his jail and I got away—that much of it is true. Rest isn't. I'm not the man he thinks I am—and that's what the sheriff'll tell him when he gets here; only I can't lay out a week in a cell."

"Which is what you're sure going to do," the deputy said. "You've got no choice."

"Even if I gave you my word not to leave the valley?"

Englund smiled. "Me take your word—word of a wanted killer? You think I'm loco?"

Starbuck shifted on the chestnut, hand inching toward his gun. "I think you're probably trying to do a job, only you've treed the wrong 'possum. I'm not Damon Friend."

"Just keep on saying it—only I know better. Jailer figures you're him, and he's seen you before. And then there's the way you do your fighting. . . . Everything tallies."

"Size—how about that?"

"Kitch says you look taller, and you ain't as heavy. Makes sense. Man losing weight would seem taller."

He had a name and now a fair description of Ben to go on—but that would be for the future. At the moment he must think of the Kelsos and Three Cross.

"Think the man you want may be my brother," Shawn said, concluding the best course to follow would be one of laying his cards on the table. It couldn't hurt, and very possibly it might set the deputy to thinking.

"I've been looking for him. Heard about a man the sheriff was hunting, came here to see if it might be him."

"But your name—you said it was Starbuck," Julie exclaimed, not fully understanding.

"It is. My brother's real name is Ben—Ben Starbuck. Description and everything you say about this Damon Friend seems to jibe, make me think they're one and the same. . . . Said when he ran off that he was going to change his name."

106

Uncertainty crossed Dave Englund's browned features and then he shook his head irritably. "Maybe so. Up to Morrison to say when he gets here."

Starbuck's level gaze locked with that of the lawman. "No, it's a decision you're making, Deputy. I can't afford to wait."

"Like I said, you ain't got no choice," Englund replied, shaking his head. "What's so all-fired important about a couple or three more days, anyhow?"

Temper flared suddenly through Shawn. "What the hell's the matter with you? Don't you ever listen? Jim Kelso's been shot, probably in danger of getting killed! Cattle are being slaughtered, fires are being set, and the way things are stacking up and—"

"Heard all that stuff, sure, but I can't—"

"And you're doing nothing about it! What's the matter with the law around here?"

"I'm following orders—Morrison's orders," Englund said doggedly. "When Kelso's got something for me to go on, I'll step in—"

"Which will be after it's too late," Julie said bitterly. "After one of us, or maybe all of us, have been killed, and the ranch is ruined. My father asked for help several times. He's never got any."

"Which is why I'm not spending one solitary hour in a cell, Deputy!" Starbuck snapped. "You won't do your job so I'm promoting myself from foreman to hired gun, and standing by these people."

"You get to slamming that iron around and—"

"I'll use it if I have to, and only because I have to," Shawn replied, glancing over the trees. The sun was down and the last light was spraying into the heavens from beyond the hills to the west, creating a vast fan of shifting color. He turned again to the lawman.

"Make you a deal. It's not safe to leave the Kelsos and Three Cross. Got a feeling that something's about to break loose—"

"Just a feeling," Englund cut in disgustedly.

"You bunk in with me for the night," Shawn continued, ignoring the deputy, "and if nothing's gone wrong by noon tomorrow, I'll admit my hunch was wrong and ride in with you."

"That's a good idea!" Julie said. "That way you'll both be on hand and—"

She paused, the distant popping of guns coming to them across the hushed, heated air. Starbuck spun, looked into

107

the direction of the ranch. A column of ugly, black smoke was spiraling into the yellowish sky.

"It's started," he said in a quick, grim voice, and digging spurs into the chestnut's flanks, sent him plunging down the grade.

= 18 =

As they drew nearer the ranch the shooting became more intense. The smoke had increased from a single streamer to three.

"Stay back!" Starbuck shouted to Julie when they broke from the trees to the south of the yard.

He drew his pistol, and threw a look at Dave Englund. The deputy had his weapon in hand, was crouched low over the saddle. Shawn glanced again to the girl as the horses pounded on. Lips compressed, eyes filled with anxiety, she gave no indication that she would obey his command.

Gunshots began to dwindle, the smoke to thicken, as they raced across the wide flat. Starbuck could see riders curving in and out of the murk that lay over the yard. The barn was blazing furiously, as were several of the small sheds. He couldn't tell if the main house or the crew's quarters had been set aflame yet or not.

He turned again to Julie, hoping she would slow, hold back, allow Englund and him to go in first. She refused to meet his eyes. Abruptly they topped the little ridge bordering the clearing in which the structures stood, and rushed into the yard. All was in chaos, utter confusion.

Four masked men were lacing back and forth, firing pistols indiscriminately. A dozen fires blazed—but Kelso's house and the low structure where the crew bunked were as yet untouched. Several Three Cross men had taken a stand inside their quarters and were returning the raiders' shots.

Starbuck saw figures lying in the swirling dust and smoke at that moment—Kelso near the kitchen shack, Aaron Lambert midway between the barn and the corrals. He heard Julie scream, was aware of her spurring past him toward her father.

Towering anger swept through him in a wild gust. Throwing himself from the chestnut, he went to one knee, leveled his pistol at the nearest shadowy figure wheeling through the pall. The bullet went true to its mark. The raider caught at his chest, then slumped forward as his horse disappeared into the gloom.

109

Englund opened up somewhere off to his left, and almost immediately a riderless horse trotted by, head up, ears pricked forward, eyes bulging with fear. Shawn, searching now for the two remaining riders, began to retreat in the direction of the house—to where he had seen Kelso sprawled. Julie would be there. He'd best get her inside and out of harm's way. He wondered where Mrs. Kelso was.

The shooting ended abruptly and a hot, pungent stillness, broken only by the crackling flames, settled over the yard. Straining his eyes to locate the outlaws, Shawn continued to back slowly for the looming bulk in the half dark that was the ranchhouse.

Shortly he saw Julie. She was to his right, her mother with her. Both were on their knees beside Jim Kelso. Even from where he crouched, several strides away, he could see that the rancher was dead. The broad stain on his chest was all the evidence needed.

He crossed hurriedly to the two women. Roughly shouldering them aside, he bent down and gathered up the rancher's body.

"Place for him's inside the house," he said, and started for the structure at a staggering run. It was the only way he knew of to get the girl and her mother under cover.

Myra Kelso hastened to get ahead of him, opened the door, and then showed the way to a corner room where Starbuck deposited the cattleman's body on a bed. He turned at once, came face to face with Julie. He studied the grief in her eyes briefly, and then with anger again soaring through him, strode for the doorway.

"Sorry—" he murmured as he brushed by her.

He neither heard nor expected an answer, simply rushed on, gun in hand, into the open. Grim, he started across the yard. Smoke and dust were beginning to dissipate, and he could make out three or four figures running back and forth from the horse trough, carrying wooden buckets filled with sloshing water as they endeavored to halt the flames threatening the cook shack.

The barn, the wagon shed, with its adjoining blacksmith's shop, several small tool and feed sheds, were still burning steadily, had been abandoned as lost. The air was hot, choking, filled with bits of floating soot and glowing sparks. He saw two men bending over Lambert, watched them pick up the old rider, start for the bunkhouse. A moment later Dave Englund, his left arm bloody and hanging stiffly at his side, appeared, followed unsteadily. One of the raiders lay nearby; there was no sign of the others.

Holstering his weapon, Shawn stepped quickly to the deputy's side, helped him into the smoke filled building. It had not been caught up by the flames but the open windows had permitted layers of drifting smoke to enter.

Ortiz, his face smeared with soot, clothes smoldering where live coals had dropped upon him, stepped back as they came through the doorway. Beyond him Pierce was working over Lambert, but there didn't appear to be much anyone could do.

Dave began to struggle with his vest and shirt, trying to work with his good arm. Shawn helped him remove the garments, and then as Pierce turned to have a look at the deputy's arm, he moved to Lambert's side, stood for a long minute staring down into the slack features of the old rider.

"Jim—they get him?"

It was Pierce asking the question. Shawn came about, nodded.

"How about his missus?"

"She's all right. Julie, too. . . . Expect we'd better get the doctor out here."

"Already sent Fermin for Ed Christie," Pierce replied, forcing Englund to a sitting position on the edge of a bunk.

Bitterness and anger suddenly overwhelmed Starbuck. "Who were they? Masked—saw that, but somebody must've recognized one of them! Was Mendoza there?"

The usually expressionless features of Isidro Ortiz tightened, and then he shrugged in a hopeless sort of way, as if decrying the all too ready practice of the *Americanos* to blame the Mexican people for such things. Shawn laid a hand on his shoulder.

"Asked that because I was talking to him earlier. He ducked out on me."

"Didn't spot him," Pierce said then. "Sure would've recognized him from what he's wearing. You saying he's mixed up in it?"

"Don't know for sure, but there's some connection," Starbuck answered, watching the old puncher dab at the puckered hole in the deputy's arm with a wad of cotton soaked in disinfectant. "Think I'll have a look at that one—"

"No need," Englund said, pushing Pierce away. "I know him. He's one of them three you claimed you'd tracked into town after the stampede. He's the one they called

111

Duncan. Expect a couple of the others were his sidekicks—Palmer and Jennings. Fourth man was Vern Ruch."

Shawn stared at the lawman as the full import of the information drilled into him. He'd been right about the three riders from the start, but that wasn't all; the fact that Omar Gentry had lied to protect them meant that they, as well as Ruch, were in his employ. Those four carried out the raid on Three Cross; it would have been at Gentry's direction.

Did that mean that Gentry was the party wanting Three Cross so badly? Was he the mysterious client that the El Paso banker, Blaisdell, represented? If so, why, why all the violence, now even death, to bring about the sale? What was the urgency, the need—the big attraction?

Starbuck stirred irritably. He was back to the puzzling question that had galled him before—only now certain things had clarified, had become definite. Gentry was a part of it. So also were Vern Ruch, Jennings, and Palmer—one of whom was badly wounded, possibly even dead. Pablo Mendoza fit into the picture somewhere, but in just what way he could not be sure.

Regardless, he knew now where to look, who to call to account not only for all the trouble that had descended upon Three Cross, but for the more serious crime of Jim Kelso and Aaron Lambert's deaths. Wheeling, he moved to the door and paused.

"Want the bunch of you to move to the main house, fort up. Don't think there'll be any more trouble but best we not take a chance."

"This here place is pretty tight for making a stand," Pierce said.

"Maybe so, but there should be somebody with the women—and it'll be better if you're all together."

Englund glanced at Starbuck's set features. "You riding into town after Ruch and the others?"

"I am—"

The deputy pulled himself to his feet. "You hold off a bit, I'll go along."

Shawn considered the lawman. He'd lost a lot of blood, was far too weak to undertake even the ride, much less a confrontation with gunmen. . . . And he knew he'd have his own hands full without being burdened with the care of the deputy.

"Be better if you stay put—"

"That's for certain," Pierce agreed. "You ain't in no shape to do much of nothing."

Englund settled back, wagged his head. "Don't hardly

112

seem right, you taking it on yourself to go after them. ....
Job for the law. Still figure you ought to wait."

Job for the law! The words echoed in Shawn's memory,
reminding him of the thought voiced only a short time
earlier by Julie Kelso, that help from that same law, when
and if it came, would be too late.

"Can't wait," he said. "Chance they may pull out, make
a run for it. .... Best I move in on them now."

=== 19 ===

Not long after midnight, Shawn Starbuck rode into Las
Cruces. The glowing anger that had gripped him was
undiminished, and there was no uncertainty in his mind as
he guided the chestnut toward the Amador Hotel.

During the crossing of the silver-flooded flats and shadowy hills that lay between Kelso's and the settlement, he'd
had time to assemble his facts and place them in orderly
fashion; he was entirely convinced that Omar Gentry was
the man solely responsible for the rancher's troubles—and
now for his death.

It would have been Gentry who made the offer to buy
Three Cross, who had hoped to speed up and guarantee
the acceptance of his proposal by making matters unten-
able for Kelso. He doubted Gentry had intended for the
rancher to be killed; it was likely an accident. There was
room for consideration there, however. Gentry could have
desired Three Cross so intensely—reason why still unknown—that he had sanctioned the murder of the rancher
feeling it would be much easier to deal with a distraught
widow.

Reason unknown. . . .

Starbuck considered that as the gelding walked softly
through the ankle-deep dust of the deserted street. He
could still find no answer to that puzzling factor, just as
Pablo Mendoza's place in the scheme was yet in darkness.
But he'd solve both questions soon; the time for settling
was at hand.

He reached the Amador, drew up to its hitchrack. The
adjoining Spanish Dagger was dimly lit, but the muffled
sound of voices and occasional bursts of laughter coming
through the open doorway attested to the presence of a
goodly number of patrons.

The hotel was dark except for a solitary lamp in the
lobby, and a lighted window on the upper floor where a
guest was apparently keeping late hours. Elsewhere the
roadway lay silent and in deep shadow—even the remaining saloons having closed for the night.

Dismounting, Shawn walked quietly to the entrance of
the Dagger. Halting in the blackness outside the door,

114

purposely propped open to trap the cooling breeze slipping down the valley from the north, he probed the faces of the men lined up at the bar, and those at the tables that fell within his range of vision.

Neither Gentry nor Ruch were to be seen. If Palmer or Jennings—whichever was alive—was there, he would have no way of knowing, since he'd never seen them except as masked riders moving in and out of the smoke and spinning dust of Kelso's yard. Jaw set, he hitched at the pistol hanging on his hip, stepped inside.

Arnie, his ruddy features drawn by a broad smile, nodded a welcome and said, "Beer, Mr. Starbuck?"

"Make it rye," Shawn replied, leaning up against the counter. Half turning, he swung his gaze over that part of the room he'd been unable to see from the street. The two he sought were not present.

The bartender slid his drink into his hands, leaned across the counter in a confidential manner. "You get all squared up with the law?"

Starbuck nodded. "Was a mistake. Deputy thought I was somebody else. . . . You see Gentry tonight?"

The saloonkeeper frowned, drew back. "Well, yes. Was in early."

Starbuck downed his drink, glanced about casually. "Don't see him now. Happen to know where he is?"

Arnie refilled the shot glass. "Couldn't say. His room, maybe, late like it is."

The bartender moved off to answer the call of another patron. Shawn emptied his glass, felt the liquor jolt some of the weariness from him. Dropping a coin on the counter, he turned away, catching Arnie's eyes on him. Nodding, he crossed the room and moved through the archway that led into the hotel. There was one room in the Amador that was lighted. Unless he was completely wrong, there was where he'd find Omar Gentry, along with Ruch and the third man, who were likely reporting the results of the raid on Three Cross.

The lobby was empty, the desk deserted, there being only a small sign next to a tap-bell, with the words *Ring For Clerk* lettered upon it to greet late arrivals. Shawn crossed to the stairway, mounted it, and made his way down the corridor until he came to a door under which a streak of light was visible.

Putting his ear to the thin panel, he listened. The clink of coins and a low mutter of voices came to him. A fresh wave of anger washed over Starbuck. Kelso dead, Aaron Lambert dead, Three Cross in charred ruins—and the men responsible callously playing cards! Drawing his pistol, he grasped the door's china knob in his right hand, and in a single movement flung the panel wide and lunged into the room.

The men at the table came to their feet in surprise. A chair overturned noisily, money clattered to the floor. Ruch reached swiftly for his weapon, froze when he saw the leveled gun.

Shawn surveyed the party coldly. Gentry, Vern Ruch, a rider who was either Jennings or Palmer, and a flashily dressed individual—one of the local gamblers, probably. Omar Gentry was the first to break the stiff silence.

"What's this all about?"

"About a raid on Three Cross—and a couple of killings."

Gentry's expression did not change. "Killings? Who?"

"Jim Kelso—and an old timer named Lambert—"

Only then did Gentry betray reaction. He flipped his cold eyes at Ruch. "You fool—" he began, and then smoothly recovered. "Wrong place, cowboy. You're looking for the deputy sheriff."

Shawn smiled quietly. He'd been right. Ruch and the others had overstepped themselves. Kelso's death had not been a part of the plan.

"I know where the deputy is—at Kelso's with a bullet in him. I'm here for you and your gun hawks."

Gentry shook his head. "Not for me. I don't know—"

"Don't play cozy with me," Starbuck cut in. "Duncan's dead. Ruch and your other hired hand there were spotted, along with the one that got a bullet in his belly."

The tall man's facade cracked slightly. "Somebody's making a mistake—"

"You've already made it," Shawn snapped. "From the start. Trying to force Kelso to sell out to you was bad enough, but killing him was the worst. . . . He was ready to accept the offer your banker friend was making for you, but you couldn't wait."

Omar Gentry said nothing, and in voicing no denial where Blaisdell was concerned, Shawn knew he'd guessed right once more.

"Want you to keep your hands up high—all of you. And turn around slow. I'm taking your guns, then we're walking over to the jail."

Alarm spread over the features of the gambler. "You got no call bringing me in on this! I don't know nothing about what you're saying. . . . Come up here to play a little stud, that's all."

116

"Tell it to the deputy," Shawn answered. "He'll be around in the morning. Get your hands up—"

"Maybe you'd best raise yours, Mr. Starbuck," Arnie's voice said from the doorway.

Shawn felt the hard muzzle of a gun press into his spine, saw relief slip into the faces of the men in front of him. Ruch immediately circled the table, a hard grin pulling at his lips. He wrenched the pistol from Starbuck's fingers and stepped back, his own weapon now out. The bartender came on into the room.

"Obliged, Arnie," Gentry said, picking up a handful of the coins lying on the table and dropping them into the saloonkeeper's vest pocket. "Appreciate this."

Arnie smiled fawningly. "Glad I could help, Mr. Gentry. Seen when Mr. Starbuck come in that he had something on his mind—asking about you and such. Then when he headed up stairs I figured I'd best have a look-see."

"Was a big favor—and I won't forget it. . . . Better get back to your customers now."

"Yes, sir, Mr. Gentry," the saloon-man said, and hurried for the door.

As he stepped into the corridor, Gentry pivoted to the gambler. "You, too, Harley—get out! And keep your mouth shut. You know what'll happen to you if you breathe one word about what happened here tonight!"

"I sure do," the gambler replied, and crossing the room quickly, also disappeared into the hall.

Ruch, Starbuck's pistol tucked under his waistband, toyed with his own weapon while keeping it pointed. "What's next?"

Gentry, features suddenly taut, whirled on the gunman. "What's next? Goddam you—I'll tell you what's next! That stupid bungling of yours is going to force us to act now!"

"Couldn't be helped. The old bastard came out shooting—"

"You should've helped it! Instead of being able to sit back, take our time like I'd planned, we'll have to grab what we can and make a run for it tonight."

"Does it make a lot of difference?"

"Makes one hell of a lot of difference. Kelso's dead—thanks to your bungling. Cat's out of the bag now. By daylight tomorrow everybody in the country'll know who did it—"

"Not if Palmer and me take this joker down the river a piece and put a bullet in his head."

"What good will that do? You heard him say the deputy

117

was at Kelso's and was in on the whole thing. And there's others besides him alive and able to talk—the women for instance. If you had to kill a couple, then you'd have been smart to kill them all so's there'd be nobody left to do any finger pointing."

Ruch was unruffled by the tongue lashing. He shrugged. "So, like I was asking—what's next?"

"We go out there tonight—right now, get what we can, and move on."

Shawn listened, realizing he was getting close to the answer he had been seeking—why Three Cross was wanted so badly by Gentry. ... But the way matters were shaping up, there was a good chance he'd not live to make use of the information.

"You want I should tie his hands?" Palmer said.

"No," Gentry replied, pulling on his hat and reaching for a leather-trimmed corduroy coat hanging against the wall. "Somebody in the saloon might notice, start wondering. Just keep up close to him—the both of you."

Starbuck, alert now for the slightest opportunity to escape, took a half step back. Ruch moved in beside him, seized him by the arm, shoved him toward the door.

"Do what you're told, *amigo*—unless you want me bending this gun barrel over your head."

Starbuck, off balance, stumbled into the corridor. Palmer and Ruch closed in beside him, and preceded by Omar Gentry, flanked by the other two outlaws, he started down the hallway. Reaching the stairs, Gentry motioned for them to wait while he took a quick glance. Finding all was clear, he beckoned them to follow, and shortly they were in the darkness of the street.

"Get the horses—the rest of the stuff, too," Gentry said, facing Palmer. "We'll wait here."

The rider turned for the stable. Shawn glanced along the row of silent buildings. There was small chance of there being anyone up and around at that hour who could help. He brought his attention back to Gentry.

"Whatever this is all about, you won't get away with it. You said it yourself—the deputy and a half dozen others know all about what happened at Kelso's. They'll be after you by daylight."

"After us, sure—but a long ways behind us. Time the sun comes up we'll be far from this burg."

"And plenty richer," Vern Ruch added with a grin.

It was the wrong thing to say. Gentry spun to the gunman. "Not rich as we ought to be—thanks to that

118

thick skull of yours! If you'd used some common sense, not acted like a stupid—"

"Easy," Ruch murmured, Gentry's lashing words finally beginning to rile him.

"It's the truth! Had it set up just right—took months— then you bungle it! Should've known you'd make a slip!"

"We can always come back—"

"With a murder charge hanging over our—my head? Stupid's not the word for you, Ruch. Ought to be a stronger one."

The gunman stiffened perceptibly. "Back off, Captain," he warned again.

Gentry, touching the outlaw with a calculating glance, shrugged, sighed deeply. "Well, no point bitching about it now. It's done, and the thing to do is get what we can." He hesitated, eyes toward the stable. "Here comes Palmer. Get this bird's horse. It's that chestnut, Vern."

Holding his own pistol on Shawn, the tall man allowed Ruch to move off, and then, smiling humorlessly, said, "You know, cowboy, I'm personally taking on the job of putting a bullet in your head. Going to be a lot of satisfaction. I worked up plenty of sweat putting this plan of mine together—and then you horned in and queered it."

"Maybe so, but mostly it was your own man, Ruch."

"Sure, but if it hadn't been for you he'd not have pulled the stupid stunt he did. You horning in got him all shook up, jumpy. . . . Wasn't for you—and him—I'd've ended up a rich man."

"Understood you already were," Starbuck said, prying, still searching for that elusive answer.

"Far from it. All show—part of the plan. You ever see an army man end up rich?"

Shawn shook his head, continued to press for the missing piece of the puzzle. "And you figured raising cattle on Kelso's place—"

Gentry snorted. "Cattle? You think that's why I was after his ranch?"

"What else?"

Omar Gentry leaned forward slightly. Light filtering from the Amador's lobby lamp glinted against his features, pointed up the strange glow in his eyes.

"Gold—"

Starbuck came up sharply. "Gold!" he echoed.

"Yes, sir—Jesuit gold," Gentry said in a taut voice. "Three chests of it buried on Kelso's property."

119

20

Jesuit gold!

Shawn stared at Gentry. That was what lay behind the man's ruthless determination to possess Three Cross! It was a bit hard to believe. He'd heard tales before of treasures buried in the New Mexico hills by priests called back to Spain by superiors who no longer trusted them, and had often wondered how much truth was in such reports. Very little, he had been assured several times.

Omar Gentry, however, didn't strike him as a man who would move on fantasy. He would be more than half sure of his information before he invested time and money in such a venture—particularly in a project where he had planned to purchase an entire ranch in order to own the property upon which the treasure was supposedly cached. His reasoning there was easy to understand; as owner of the land anything found on it was legally his.

"Mount up," he heard Gentry say.

Moving to the chestnut, he went to the saddle, noting the two shovels and several pairs of saddlebags Palmer had brought with the horses.

"Best we get right along," Gentry continued. "Not much time left before daylight, and we want to be gone by then."

Ruch nodded, jerked his thumb at Starbuck. "What about him? Ought to shuck him somewheres so's we won't be bothered."

Omar Gentry grinned. "Got plans for him. Being big and strong—he'll do the digging for us. Can get rid of him after that."

The gunman signified his approval of the idea. "Glad to hear that. These here hands of mine never did fit no shovel."

They moved out at once, striking due west for the river, fording it almost directly opposite the settlement. There, with Palmer forging out to take the lead, they angled off through the short hills, keeping to a trail that ran parallel to, but was somewhat above the road Shawn and Jim Kelso had taken that first day.

As they rode steadily on through the cool night, Starbuck tried to look ahead, prepare for an attempt to escape. Chances weren't good, he had to admit. Palmer was in front of him, Gentry and Ruch, riding side by side, were at his back. At any effort to make a break they could easily shoot him out of the saddle.

But to delay until they reached their destination would be pressing his luck to the limit. He had no inkling of where the gold was buried, but there was little doubt in his mind that any opportunity to get away would be served best along the brush-lined trail. . . . He must somehow distract the two outlaws behind him, buy a fleeting moment of chance.

"Heard about Jesuit gold," he said, twisting about on the gelding. "Always figured it was just talk."

Gentry shrugged. "Most tales are. This isn't."

"Expect every man who goes looking for it feels the same way."

"Not every man gets his hands on what I did—a letter telling all about a treasure. Even the Mexican government's heard of the one I'm—we're—after. They just didn't know where the cache is."

"A letter—not a map?" Shawn was putting the question to Gentry but his eyes were on Vern Ruch. The gunman appeared to be dozing.

"What I said. Maps are usually not worth the paper they're scribbled on. What I got my hands on was a letter from some family in Spain to an old *padre* living near Chihuahua. Was a relative, I suppose. Told all about the treasure three Jesuits had buried. He was to turn it over to the government, help pay for the war Benito Juarez had been fighting against the French."

"But he gave it to you instead—"

Gentry smiled, obviously enjoying the recounting of his ingenuity. "Not exactly. Might say I relieved him of it. . . . I'd been down there, helping Juarez run his army ever since our war ended in sixty-five. Was no problem for me."

"Then you came up here, located the treasure, and when you found out it was on private land, started trying to buy it. That about three months ago—when you had Blaisdell make Kelso that offer?"

The tall man laughed. "You've got yourself in the wrong calling, friend. Instead of a cowhand you ought to be a detective—like one of those Pinkerton agents. . . . Yeh, I had Blaisdell make an offer—legitimate and on the level, too. Just good poker playing to lay out a couple of thousand dollars to win back twenty or thirty times that much—in gold."

"Kelso would have never sold that cheap."

"When I got through with ragging him, he'd likely have sold for less. Got a feeling he'd just about reached that point—only Ruch, there, had to go and foul everything up with that damned gun of his. . . . Have to grab what I can of the gold now. Maybe I can come back in a few years when it's all forgot, dig up the rest."

"If it's there at all."

Gentry spat. "It's there. No if nor ands about this treasure. Fact is, the Mexican government's got a man here right now, watching me, hoping I'll tip him off. The old *padre* wasn't dead as I thought, seems."

"A *vaquero* by the name of Mendoza—he the agent you mean?"

"That's him. Poor bastard—sure have led him a long chase, and he's no closer right now to getting that gold than he was in Chihuahua."

That accounted for Pablo Mendoza, Shawn thought, settling back. A representative of the Mexican government; it explained his hanging around, watching, waiting, patrolling the valley. He was simply keeping an eye on Gentry, hoping the man would make his move.

"Ought to be about there," Ruch said, shifting on his saddle. The gunman had not been as unaware of things as he had wanted others to believe, apparently. "Good thing. We sure ain't going to have much time."

"Thanks to you—" Gentry snapped.

Starbuck was looking over the shadowy land, striving to recall the terrain, the location of the arroyos, the deeper ravines, but his knowledge of the area was scant. If he were to make a move toward escaping, however, it should be soon; the brush bordering the trail would afford him excellent cover—if he could reach it before a bullet cut him down.

Palmer, quickening the pace despite the roughness of the path, began to veer right. Shortly the shaded depths of a small, steep-walled canyon came into view. Shawn strained to see the floor of the declivity, to determine the nature of its floor. If it was smooth and sandy, he could risk jumping the chestnut down into it. Cluttered with rocks and brush, it would be foolhardy—and fatal.

After a few moments he gave it up. It was impossible to tell what lay below. He'd have to come up with something else.

"Rider coming—"

At Palmer's low-pitched warning, Gentry stopped. Instantly Vern Ruch spurred to Starbuck's side, jammed a pistol against his back.

"One sound, cowboy, and you're dead!"

Shawn heard it then, the light but steady *tunk-a-tunk* of a horse coming down the trail toward them.

"Some drifter," Ruch murmured.

"Maybe," Gentry answered at low breath. "Pull off into that brush ahead of you. We'd best wait and see. Can't afford any more mistakes."

Ruch dug the pistol's muzzle deeper into Starbuck, kneed the chestnut into a thick stand of false mahogany immediately to their right. Palmer dropped back, joined them.

"Mind what I said," the gunman again warned Shawn.

Starbuck barely heard. Ruch was close. He could see the handle of his own pistol sticking up from the outlaw's waistband where it had been thrust. It was less than an arm's length away—available and tempting.

"Here he comes," Palmer whispered, and then added, "It's that Mex—"

In that fragment of time, Shawn Starbuck elected to gamble, make his try. His hand shot out, jerked the pistol from Ruch's waistband.

"Mendoza—look out!" he yelled, and firing point blank at the gunman, threw himself backwards into the brush.

The gelding reared in sudden fright, long fore legs striking out, slashing at the horse Ruch was riding. Gentry yelled something. Two quick gunshots crashed as Shawn hit the solidness that was the slope of the little canyon, and went plunging on to the bottom.

Instantly he veered to the side, began to claw his way through a band of scrub oak, knowing that he must get away from the point where he had dropped from the outlaw's sight. He could see the chestnut outlined against the sky above him, along with another horse. Ruch's likely. Nothing else was in view—and there was only silence.

He paused, began to proceed more cautiously. What had happened to Gentry and Palmer? And Mendoza? Ruch was down, undoubtedly dead; he couldn't have missed a fatal shot at such close range. . . . Those two other reports—did they indicate an exchange between the *vaquero* and Gentry, or possibly Palmer? Had any of them been hit?

He gained the top of the deep slash. The trail was only a step or two ahead in the open. It looked like a silver band in the starlight—soft and deadly. Crouched, he waited, listened, swinging his attention from right to left. The chestnut, and Ruch's bay, were now off to one side grazing amiably on the clumps of bunchgrass.

Where the hell was everybody?

He sweated out another long minute and then, impatient but careful, flat on his belly, he began to crawl toward the horses.

"*Senor—*"

Mendoza's hushed summons came from the brush on the opposite side of the trail.

"Here."

"You are not injured?"

"No. . . . How about you?"

"A bullet in the leg. It is nothing."

Shawn remained silent for several moments, listening into the night. There was nothing except the cropping sound the horses were making. Evidently they had not been overheard.

"There's two of them left," he said then. "You happen to see which way they ducked?"

"Into the brush, I do not know exactly where. The man Gentry is one."

"Yeh, Gentry and Palmer."

The outlaws were simply waiting for them to show themselves, Starbuck realized. . . . He'd oblige them but not in the way they hoped.

"Can you walk, *amigo?*" he called in a whisper.

"Oh, yes. The wound is small. You wish for me to come there?"

"No. . . . Expect they're hiding in that thick brush to the left of the horses, hoping we'll step out and give them a couple of easy pot shots. You keep low, work in from that direction. I'll do the same on this side. . . . Ready?"

"*Si, caporal*, I am ready."

At once, Starbuck began to make his way through the tough oak bushes, keeping as flat to the ground as was humanly possible. Across the way he could hear a faint scraping as Mendoza kept abreast.

He paused, sweating even in the night's coolness, brushed at his eyes to clear the moisture. Careful, he raised his head. The gelding was only a few strides away. He saw Ruch then, stretched out at the edge of the trail, face down. Dropping low again, he continued.

Abruptly a shadow raised up before him. Starlight glinted off metal. Instinctively Shawn threw himself to one side, triggered a shot from a prone position. Almost in the identical breath, two quick reports blasted along the opposite side of the trail.

Rolling to one knee, Starbuck hung there in the darkness while the echoes bounced through the night. A groan came to him through the pungent, drifting wisps of smoke.

"Mendoza?"

"Here, *senor*. I—I have had the bad luck again. Come—there is no danger. I see the *cabrones*. They will trouble no man again."

Starbuck leaped to his feet, crossed the path, and hesitated. Glancing about he located the *vaquero*, quickly knelt beside him. Mendoza had taken a bullet in his chest. An arm's length away Omar Gentry lay on his back, sightless eyes staring up into the star-spattered sky. Evidently the two men had all but collided in the dark, and both had fired together. . . . A short distance to the left Palmer, the shadow that had risen in his path, lay draped over a fallen tree.

"Best I get you to the doc," Shawn said. "Like as not he's still at Kelso's."

Mendoza gestured feebly with his hand. "There is no need. I rest well here and would stay. We are men, *compadre*. We know death has come for me."

Shawn lowered his head. "Afraid so. . . . I'm sorry."

"Do not be. I am pleased for I have finished the job my government sent me to do. I have prevented this man Gentry from finding the gold that belongs to my country, the *Gorgojo* treasure."

"The what?"

"*Gorgojo*—a word that makes little meaning. It is the name given to the treasure by a dying man—a priest slain by Gentry for a letter he carried. It was one that told of the gold."

"There an English word for it?"

"This I do not know. In the language of my people it refers to a small worm, one found in meal."

"A weevil," Shawn supplied. "You're right, it doesn't make much sense. We were going after the gold when we ran into you."

Mendoza stirred hopefully. "Then the location of this treasure is known to you?"

"Afraid not. Gentry never told me. Don't think the others knew either. Somewhere on Kelso's ranch is about as close as I can get."

The *vaquero* settled back. For a time the only sound was his labored breathing and then, managing a shrug, he said: "It is sad. My people are very poor, starving from the time of the war. They are in need of the simplest of things, and have great need of the gold which was taken from them by the Jesuits."

Mendoza paused, breathing hard. He clutched at Starbuck's arm, lifted his head slightly. His eyes were bright. "A promise, *senor!* Tell the *senora*—the woman of Kelso of the treasure. Beg of her in the name of sacred charity to find this treasure of Gorgojo, return it to my people who are the rightful owners. . . . Do this for me, I ask it of you!"

Shawn clasped the *vaquero's* hand firmly, nodded. "You've got my word on it."

"It is enough," Mendoza sighed, his lips parting in a faint smile.

"If she's willing, I'll do some scouting around the hills, see if I can turn up—"

Starbuck's words drifted into nothingness as a sudden thought, like a shaft of penetrating light, ripped into his mind, sent a tremor racing through him. . . . Three graves that, perhaps, were not graves at all; three crosses on a hill that could have been meant to serve as markers for men who planned one day to return but never did—and a strange word—*gorgojo*—that lacked meaning.

Could the mumbled words of the dying priest been misunderstood? Could he have, instead, muttered the name, *Golgotha*—another hill in a far away land where centuries ago there also had stood three crosses? That must have been the way of it! The Jesuits had designated the location of their buried treasure by drawing an obvious but unsuspected parallel.

Shawn bent over the dying man. "Mendoza—listen to me. . . ."

The Mexican stirred weakly. His eyes opened and the smile again crossed his lips. *"Adios, compadre."*

Starbuck looked more closely at him. It was too late. "So long, my friend," he said quietly.

"Vaya con Dios," the *vaquero* murmured and fell silent.

Pablo Mendoza would never know that the treasure he sought, and wanted returned to his people so badly, had been found.

21

The chests were there, as Shawn had been certain they would be, buried deep beneath the piles of stone that marked the location of each cross. He had explained it all to Myra and Julie Kelso and they agreed it rightfully belonged to Mexico and should be returned.

To avoid political complications, Starbuck, with a dozen special deputies under the direction of Sheriff Abel Morrison, transported the treasure—mostly jeweled church vessels, chalices, crosses, and crucifixes inlaid with precious stones, and a good-sized amount of gold coin, to the border, where it was handed over to a small army dispatched to meet them by Pablo Mendoza's superiors.

Now, astride the chestnut gelding, Starbuck paused on the summit of a hill east of Three Cross, and in the clean, crisp sunlight of New Year's Day, looked back to the ranch. He raised his arm in farewell. Julie Kelso, standing in the center of the yard, lifted her hand in reply.

Everything had worked out. Morrison had cleared him of the murder charge the deputy had lodged against him, had in addition supplied him with all the information he could muster concerning Damon Friend—who unquestionably was Ben. The accusation against his brother would stand, however, the lawman told him; but it was a matter that could be cleared up if Ben would return and face trial.

The Kelsos, mother and daughter, had recovered from the loss of Jim as well as could be expected in that short time, and were planning to continue raising cattle.

Sitting motionless there on the saddle, eyes roving moodily the broad swale in which the ranch lay, now a pale, sage green under winter's touch, Shawn sighed regretfully. . . . He could have remained as foreman, run Three Cross as if it were his own, but he knew it wasn't possible. It would never be until he found Ben.

Thus he was moving on, just as he had told Jim Kelso he would when the first day of the new year came. He had gained far more than needed wages during his stay; he had a description of, as well as a name for his brother. And while the frontier into which Ben had disappeared was no smaller than it had been in the beginning, he now possessed that first link with which to build a chain. Perhaps he'd find the second in Texas.